Twelve Rounds of Love

Donna Plata

DEDICATION

This book is dedicated to all the women, men, and children who have lost their lives as a result of Domestic Violence.

ACKNOWLEDGEMENTS

First and foremost, I would like to thank God for giving me the talents that have allowed me to be a blessing to others. I am extremely grateful for all that He's done for me.

Furthermore, I am thankful for my family and friends who support me in my endeavors. My husband; Mike, and our children; Lavell, Michael Jr, De'Marco, and Mariya have always been there to encourage me to pursue my passions. I appreciate my parents Saundra and Mark, as well as my in laws, Gerri and Michael, for always loving me.

Lastly, I want to extend a special thank you to my editor and friend, Yara Kaleemah as she has been there since day one. I cannot thank you enough for making my books what they are. I appreciate you.

Twelve Rounds of Love

Donna Plata

Chapter One

A light drizzle dropped from the cloudy New York City sky as Angel and Carla shared a light meal at their favorite restaurant, Belle's Blues. Angel leaned back in her seat, scrolling over her Facebook Timeline.

"I just want to meet a nice guy and settle down. I mean is that too much to ask?" She pouted.

"No, it's not Angel, but you got to be willing to put in time and effort to build a relationship."

"Ugh ain't nobody got time for all that." She chuckled. "I'm ready to get married have babies and live my happily ever after."

"OK see now you're living in a fairytale." Carla laughed, taking a sip of her drink.

"I'm just kidding," Angel said as she taps her shoulder "You know what I mean. I just don't want to start all over have to do the whole dating process all over again."

"I mean that's what it's going to take unless you trying to find some random ass nigga to have a baby with." Carla rolled her eyes.

"Hell naw." Angel placed the phone on the table and searched for something in her purse.

"Ok then like I said you got to be willing to put the time and effort in. Anything worth having is worth fighting for. So, if that's what you want you got to put your gloves on."

"Well shit I'm bout to knock a couple people out then." Angel shrugged.

Carla smiled. "Don't hurt 'em."

Carla and Angel continued with light conversation, laughs, and full bellies. Angel looked at her watch realizing that she needed to be home in time to catch up on her shows. Keys in hand, she and Carla headed for the parking lot. Damn, Angel thought getting a whiff of the gentleman's cologne as he passed them. He was tall, dark, and bearded. It was a bushy beard that matched his eyebrows and lips.

"You're leaving already, Queen?" Mr. Dark and Lovely asked as he grabbed Angel's hand but, she snatched away.

"Yes, we are. Thank you very much." Angel smirked.

"Dang I was just hoping to get a little of your time; no disrespect."

"None taken, but my girl and I were just leaving." Carla interjected.

"Carla?"

"What? Angel we were."

"I know but we ain't gotta rush." Angel spoke through clenched teeth and a smile. "Listen my girl and I were just leaving but we can exchange numbers to keep in touch."

"That's straight." He smiled, too, as they each pulled out their phones. "Well hit me up when you free."

"Alright I will." She and Carla walked out.

"What was that?"

"What?"

"Didn't you say if it was worth having it was worth fighting for?"

"Ugh I meant a relationship not a one-night stand."

"Who says I won't call him afterwards?" Angel laughed.

"Girl you a mess." Carla laughed, unlocking her car.

Chapter Two

Angel stared up at the ceiling as she laid in her California King Size bed. She scrolled through Instagram and then through Facebook. Fuck, I'm bored. She snapped her teeth and flicked through the Firestick. Nothing popping on Facebook and ain't shit to watch on this TV. Hum, Angel remembered o' boy from the restaurant. That nigga was smelling like a whole fucking snack! She quickly pulled up his number and shot a quick text. Her heart was fluttering and shit like a young ass girl while she waited for him to hit her line back.

Beep.

Oh shit! She thought, reading his reply. Apparently, he had been waiting on her text. She was grinning like a little school girl until her phone started ringing. At first, she thought it was him, but it was one of her home girls.

"What up, doe?" Angel asked.

"Hey girl what you doing?"

"Nothing much, texting this dude I met the other day."

"Who?"

"Some dude named Daniel."

She laughed, "That's a corny ass name."

"Bitch bye. I bet his money long though." Angel shook her head and checked if he sent a message.

"He got any friends?"

"Look at you," she laughed, "I don't know, he had a couple with him I couldn't see what they look like."

"What were they wearing masks?" she said sarcastically.

"No but you know Carla she damn near yanked my arm off trying to get me out the door."

"Damn, but yeah that's your girl. You know how she is she don't like hood niggas. Well did you at least get a look at him?"

"Girl yes and yes he was fine."

You know fine niggas run in packs and I need me a fine nigga."

"Alright, I'll see if he got any single friends."

"Single? Hell, I don't care if they married shit. I need a nigga to give me a couple ends when I need it. Lil dick here and there."

"Bitch bye!"

"What? Side bitches need love too."

"Girl bye. I'ma call you back in a lil while. I gotta go check on this laundry." Angel laughed; black people say anything to get off the damn phone.

"Alright."

Angel responded to Daniel's last two messages and started looking through Netflix again. She just knew she was about to be somewhere Netflix and Chillin with Daniel fine ass in a minute. She shrugged, knowing that Carla's ass would not approve. But who gave a fuck? Now was the time to live. Hell, I'm still young. Angel shook her head.

"Are you busy?" Angel texted.

"Never too busy for a beautiful woman." He quickly replied.

She was smiling from ear to ear. She could dang near feel that big ass bushy beard rubbing on her thighs. She squeezed her legs together and typed a response.

"Haven't been called Beautiful in a minute."

"Unless you changed your appearance since the last time I saw you I call it like I see it."

"Well thank you for that compliment you made my day."

"Well let me make it even better. You wanna go out tonight?"

"Sure, but first do you have a girlfriend? Wife? Or crazy baby mama?" Angel laughed as she hit send.

" LOL. Naw none of those. I'm clean."

"Ok cool cause I don't like drama. Oh, do you have any friends my home girl could hook up with? Oops did that sound desperate? Cause she would kill me."

"Yeah, it did. Naw I'm just kidding but, yeah I got a couple cats I can introduce her to."

"Okay good looking and don't tell her I said it."

He laughed. "I won't. Now how you want to do this? You wanna roll solo or we coupling up?"

"Either way sounds like a plan."

"Alright I'll holla around 7:30 to 8:00"

"Okay. Now let me call and see if she's up for the challenge."

Angel called Trina back. "Ayo," Angel said when she finally answered. "Alright he gone call me around 7:30 to see what's up."

"What you mean what's up?"

"If his boy wanna hook up with you or not."

"Bitch! Don't be making me out to be no charity case."

"I didn't." Angel tried not to laugh.

Trina rolled her eyes on the other side of the phone. She needed a little boo but not that badly. "Bitch you did. Talking bout whether his boy wanna hook up with me or not."

"Well I ain't mean to say it that way. Girl I know you're the baddest bitch." Angel laughed.

"You better say it cause I'm always together. Well most of the time you know I'm a baller on a budget. That's why I'm looking for a meal ticket." Trina admitted as she filed her nails.

Angel burst into laughter, "I can't stand you. I cannot take you seriously at all."

"Well you better hope oh boy can come through or you'll be taking me to dinner. Talking bout you can't take me serious. Ha alright call me and let me know." Trina rolled her eyes.

"Okay, I will." Angel hung up, thinking about what she was going to wear.

Angel got up, cleaned up her apartment, freshened up

and chilled. She passed time by watching TV and surfing the net. As the time went by she started getting butterflies in the pit of her stomach. She was excited but nervous all she wanted to do was have a boyfriend and it's been about six months since she's been with a man. Her time was long overdue, and she knew she deserved to be happy and wanted nothing more but to be able to call someone hers. Her phone rang.

"Hello." She tried to hide her excitement.

"What's up Angel? How we looking tonight?" From the sound of his voice she knew some bullshit was about to pop off.

Angel frowned because she knew he was about to say something stupid. "Everything good on my end what's up with you?"

"Well I got good news and I got bad news. Which one you want first?"

"The bad news cause I'm gone need the good news to soothe it over." Angel sighed, awaiting a long story.

"Well the bad news is I'm not going to be able to make it." Daniel told her, sensing her disappointment.

Angel sucked through her teeth. Why the fuck did I even call this nigga? She rolled her eyes and leaned back on the couch. I shoulda' known he was full of shit.

"Well what's the good news?" She asked.

"Your girl got a date for tonight. I know this isn't a good first impression but if you let me make it up to you I promise I will." Daniel tried to make her feel better.

"I can't be upset anyway because we didn't officially make plans, but yeah you can make it up to me." Angel smirked.

"Alright bet I got you grab a pen and paper take down homeboy's number and give it to your girl." He said,

"I can put it in my phone, what is it?" Angel put him on speaker to type the number into her phone.

After Daniel gives her the number, they hung up. Angel shot Trina the number in a text and then, called her.

"Hello?" Trina answer.

"What's up Tee?" Angel held the phone on her shoulder while she poured a glass of Long Island Ice Tea. "OK Daniel called and gave me his boy phone number to give to you. You got my text."

"Yea, I got it but wasn't we possed to go out together?" Trina asked, curiously.

"Nah, oh boy canceled." Angel took a sip of her drink. "Asshole."

" That's some bullshit. I ain't bout to meet up with this nigga alone. You watch Catfish, don't you?"

Angel laughed, "You crazy as hell, chile."

"Uh uh you gone be the third wheel tonight, Bitch!" Trina laughed.

"Why I got to go with y'all? I ain't gone have nobody to be all caked up with."

"And neither will I if this nigga ugly, ain't got no money, no teeth, cock eyed, pigeon-toed or shorter than me." Trina was dead serious she was not about to be dealing with no basket case. She was all about finding a nigga with a little bit of dough, not no Coney Island funnel cake dough but some let's catch a flight type of nigga.

"You are so silly I swear." Angel shook her head.

"I'm so serious, I swear. Well at least come wherever we meeting up at just in case I need you."

Angel smacked her lips, "Ugh."

"I mean you ain't doing nothing else might as well come out and hang out." Trina urged.

"Alright you call him, and I'll get ready."

After hanging up with her girl, Angel sighs, taking another drink. She was sad that she couldn't seem to find a good dude. She was mentally and sexually frustrated. All she really wanted was some good dick. She didn't really need the strings, especially since Malcom's ass went to jail. She remembered all the nights she had laid in bed crying and then, finally his ass was hauled off to jail. She took another gulp of Long Island.

"Why can't I have happiness? Where is My One True Love? One who's destined to be with me? Maybe I'm just fooling myself. I mean what did I expect?" Angel carried the cup into the living room with her phone in the other hand.

Trina called her to let her know what was going on with her and Daniel's homie.

"Hello?" Angel plopped down on the couch.

"Yeah, girl. Ok, so he's meeting me at Motor City." She said.

Angel curled up her bottom lip. "Motor City?"

"Yeah that way we can eat and still get our party on. And push comes to shove if he not to my liking I can get a rebound." Trina said as a matter of fact.

"I can't with you," Angel shook her head. "Alright what time?"

"9." Trina answered.

"I'll be there."

Angel lit a few candles and ran a hot bath. She needed to relax and get over the fact that Daniel stood her up. Hell, he got a lot of making up to do, she thought as she slid into the water. Suddenly her phone buzzed interrupting her favorite Usher song. Damn, she dried her hand and answered.

"Yerdie, Carla." She sang into the phone.

"Yerdie? Girl, I am not one of your hood ass friends." Carla snapped her teeth.

"Oh, shut up," Angel laughed. "Prude ass."

Carla rolled her eyes. She was trying to teach Angel that a good man wanted a girl with a good mouth, literally and figuratively. "Ugh, chile. What you doing?"

"In the tub." Angel ran her hands over her nipples,

thinking about Daniel sucking on them.

"Yeah, clean that pussy." Carla laughed.

Angel frowned. "Oh, shit you said P-U-S-S-Y."

They both laughed at Carla's expense. "Anyway, what you getting into tonight?"

"Well," Angel sighed. "I was hooking up with that guy Daniel from the other day. He called to say he couldn't make it, but I was able to hook Trina up with one of his homeboys."

"So, what? You're feeling down about it?"

"Yes, I mean when is it gone be my turn? You have your fancy lawyer husband. Trina has her many of men. What do I have? Bob on occasions and that's when the battery is not dead."

"Girl please, Antwan is a lawyer but he still from MLK." Carla laughed. "You can take them out the hood but the hood always going to be in them." She laughed.

"Girl, ain't that the truth." Angel laughed, too. "But we know you like them tamed dudes." She joked.

"Angel don't judge by our lives or anyone else's. When the right man comes along you'll know it."

"Easy for you to say you got a man." Angel shrugged.

Carla was always trying to be so positive; inspirational. Sometimes Angel wondered how they had remained friends all these years. Carla was a college graduate and she went to church every Sunday. She was different and didn't really like to mesh with hood chicks but somehow, she and Angel had grown to be really good friends. It seemed to be a mystery. Angel rolled her eyes, knowing that everyone wasn't meant to meet Prince Charming. That shit only came once in a life time and Angel's time was running out. She stood up in the tub and wrapped a thick white towel around her body.

"And I always had him, haven't I? You remember those late nights we used to go out looking for someone to buy our drinks?"

"Yeah and now you got a man to do that." Angel walked into her bedroom and opened the closet door.

"Angel when I met Antwan do you remember what I told you?" Carla asked.

Angel pulled out three dresses and placed them on the bed. "What?"

"That I was gone stop looking for a man and let my man find me. I had to work on me and learn my worth before I gave a man my heart." Carla explained.

"Blah blah blah Carla, ain't nobody trying to hear all that. I'm over here lonely as hell miserable and horny as fuck. I ain't had none in six months." Angel shook her head.

Carla sighed. "Your Mr. Right will come along Angel."

Just then her other line clicked. She looked at the phone and smiled.

"Saved by the bell hold on." Angel said as she put her on hold. "Hello?"

"What up Angel? Is that offer still on the table?" Daniel asked in a sweet voice. "For me to make it up to you?"

"Uhm yeah hold on." She clicked back over to Carla. "Forget all that stuff I said I got myself a date."

"With who? Cause that was fast." Carla laughed.

"Daniel, he's on the other end so I'll call you back later better, yet I'll call you tomorrow."

"Alright bye." Carla hung up.

"Hello." She took him off hold.

"You did say 'yes', didn't you?"

"Of course, I did. I was going to go out with my girl when you reschedule."

"Oh, is that right?" Daniel asked. "Where?"

"Motor City." Angel said, trying to decide which dress she was going to put on.

"Oh, that's the spot." Daniel said, excitedly.

"Yeah what I look like sitting in the house on a Friday

night?"

"Right that's what I'm saying let's get you out the house."

"Sounds like a plan. Let me toss on some clothes." Angel told him.

"Okay so how you want to do it? You want me to scoop you?"

"Nah, I will meet you there at 9."

"Alright see you then." They hung up.

A navy-blue dress hugged all of Angel's curves and silver jewelry brought out the highlights in her skin. She draped a black shoulder bag on her arm and held her pumps until she got to the front door of her apartment. Looking around the living room, she turned off the lights and stepped out of the door. As she approached the front door of the three story walk up, she pulled out her keys and a small bottle of hair spray. It was illegal to carry mace, so it would have to do if a nigga tried to act crazy. She popped the locks to her Honda Accord and slid into the driver's seat. Dammit, she snapped her teeth as the phone rang.

"I'm bout tired of this fucking phone." Angel looked to see who it was. Seemed like she had spent the better part of the evening on the phone. She rolled her eyes as she answered.

It was Trina, she answered as she revved the engine, "What's up?"

"Hey girl change of plans we left the club." Trina chuckled.

"Dang we was on our way up there." Angel snapped her teeth. "Where y'all at now?"

"At his house I'll tell you all about it tomorrow."

"What?" Angel snapped her teeth. "What is up with you?"

Trina giggled as the drinks started to set in. Jesse, Daniel's homie, was nibbling on her ear and squeezing her breast while she talked to Angel on the phone. He put his hand between her thighs and tickled her clit. She could hardly contain herself.

"Bye Bitch!" Trina hung up the phone.

"Did this heffa just hang up on me? Unbelievable." Angel shook her head and called Daniel back.

"Yo?" he answered.

Angel looked in the rear-view mirror and said, "Yeah that's a no go they left the club."

"Yeah my boy just called and told me. So, what you wanna do?"

Hesitantly she replied, "Ugh! Send me the address I'm on my way."

"Alright bet."

Angel arrived at Daniel's house and was diffident to get out of the car and walk up to the door. He looked out the window to see her sitting there and waved for her to come in. She watches ID channel way too much to be trusting some dude she just met. She imagined him holding her hostage and stabbing her twenty times. Hell, she thought, pulling out her phone. She texted the address to Carla just in case something happened to her. She shook her head and tried to calm her nerves as she reached for her purse and climbed out of the car.

It was a tidy little apartment with hardwood floors and accent art work on the walls. It smelled good too. He had shoe boxes piled up against one wall and the other wall was covered with CD's. Angel was surprised she hadn't seen an actual CD in years. There was a brown leather sectional sofa and a 62" TV mounted to the wall.

"You have a nice place for a guy." Angel took her shoes off and placed them on the mat at the door.

"Thanks, I think." Daniel shrugged looking down at her shoeless feet. "Uh, you didn't have to take your shoes off."

"No, it's habit. My parents never let us walk around the

house in our outside shoes. My dad believed it brings in the evil of the outside."

"So, what about your dress?" Daniel smirked.

Angel rolled her eyes, "Funny, smart ass." She sat on the couch and he sat next to her.

"Are you nervous being here with me?"

"Why you say that?"

"Cause you sat all the way on the other end of the couch."

"Psst naw I'm good. I'm not nervous. I'm good." Angel frowned.

Daniel stood up and walked over to the bar on the other side of the room. "Hold on let me fix you a drink to calm your nerves."

"Is it that obvious?" Angel took a deep breath.

"Yeah it is." He chuckled.

"I'm sorry it's just been a minute since I been on a date."

"Aww it no thang just like riding a bike."

They shared a laugh and Angel started to loosen up with that drink in her system. Later on, that night, she got to dancing on him rubbed her hands up and down his arms. He kissed her neck and she paused.

"What's wrong?"

"Nothing it's just been so long."

"Well just go with the flow."

He started kissing her again she climbed on his lap and straddled him on the couch. Daniel slid his hand up under her shirt and started rubbing her titties. Angel put her hand on his lap and started rubbing between his legs feeling his penis bulge through his pants. She started rocking back and forth grinding on him.

"Do you want to see it?" he smirked.

Angel licked her lips in anticipation. It had been so long since she had seen a live dick. Watching porn and fingering herself was not getting it anymore. She yearned to ride a thick piece of flesh and hoped that Daniel ass was packing. Hell, at this point she would be willing to fuck him even if it wasn't as big as expected.

"Yes," she whispered, biting her lip.

He pulled it out and she leaned back looking down at it. Damn, her eyes got wide as she sized it up. He was thick, long and shiny. Her pussy was throbbing at thought of him being deep inside of her. She leaned forward and kissed Daniel on the neck.

"Don't be scared, he don't bite." Daniel grinned.

Angel's lips danced on his neck, the side of his face and then, she sucked on his ear. His hands were roaming on her body while she repositioned herself on his lap. His head laid back on the couch as she wrapped her arms around his neck. Their lips locked in a succulent kiss that made her panties wet. Angel rubbed her pussy against his thickening manhood, brushing her titties against his mouth. "Damn, baby," Daniel groaned.

Angel stood up in front of him, looking down at his sexy ass biceps and hardened nipples. She pulled her dress up slightly above her hips and put one foot on the edge of the couch. He was staring up at her as she pushed her panties to the side and gently rubbed her clit. A moan escaped her lips as Daniel reached around and squeezed her ass cheeks. Her juices were dripping down her leg and he couldn't take it anymore. So, he stood up, swooping her into his arms and carried her in to the bedroom. He laid her down on the bed and spread her legs apart. Angel arched her back, staring at the wall on the other side of the room. His warm mood caressed her entire pussy, sucking it like a nectarine.

"Oh shit," she screeched, her legs quivering. "Dan…. Daniel."

His tongue was twirling around her clit, flicking in with tension. Then, he put one finger in her pussy and the other in her ass. Angel grunted with excitement and surprise. Met with intense pleasure, her legs were now shaking out of control. She was trying to keep up, not knowing which way to grind.

"Damn," she yelled pressing her ass down hard on his hand.

She could have never imagined that anal penetration would get her so hot. Finally, a wet nut spattered on his face, but he was not done. He slurped on her pussy so hard she thought her cervix was going to pop out. Then he pushed her body to the edge of the bed and her head was dangling off. He walked around the bed and dropped his pants; his dick slang out and hit her on the chin. Angel opened her mouth wide and took in most of him. She held on to his hips as he moved in and out of her mouth. The rush she felt was unlike anything she had ever been through. He reached over and rubbed on her clit while she squeezed the tip of his dick with her mouth. He stood up on his tippy toes and rocked back and forth until his dick jerked. He pulled it out of her mouth and busted on her chest.

"Get up," he demanded and helped her into a doggy style position.

"Wait…" Angel said.

"What's the matter," Daniel frowned.

"You got a condom?"

"Oh, iight." He dug in his pants and hastily put on a Magnum.

He slid right into that wet-wet. Angel was throwing it back like she was on a horse. He held on to her hips on his toes while she grabbed on the sheets. He pounced on her, thrusting in and out until he felt her tightening her pussy on him.

"Oh shit! Oh shit!" Angel yelled as he pushed his thump into her ass. "Oh shit, I'ma cum!"

"That's right! Come on Daddy dick! Cum for me!" Daniel smacked her on the ass and grabbed her by the back of the neck. "Cum! Cum, Angel!"

Angel let out a loud grunt and plopped down on the bed. She rolled over and Daniel sat next to her. Hell, that was a fucking work out. They were both huffing and puffing. He rubbed her stomach and gazed into her eyes.

"Damn, baby." He kissed her on the cheek.

Angel smiled, shyly. "It was popping, wasn't it?"

"Don't go getting all big headed and shit."

"Fuck you mean?" she sat up on her elbows. "I gave it to your ass."

"Man, shut up before I fuck you in the ass." He joked.

"In the ass? Nah nah nah!" Angel laughed. "Go get me a rag or something."

Daniel left the room and she laid there gathering her thoughts and her pussy. She was still throbbing and a part of her hoped that he would come back in the room and fuck her two days from Sunday, again. She was grinning like a little virgin. *Damn that nigga know how to lay the pipe; fuck around and have my ass in love and shit. I usually don't fuck niggas like that on the first date but there is something different about his fine ass.*

Daniel came back into the room with a small bucket of water and a rag. Angel looked at him like he was crazy as hell.

"What you don't trust me to wash my own ass? Or you got another bitch shit in your bathroom?" she cut her eyes at him.

"Nah, nothing like that but I just thought after the way I just fucked you, you might not make it to the bathroom." He grinned.

He pulled her legs apart and started to wash her and then, told her to slide up on the bed. He turned on the TV and laid next to her. This was some totally different shit!

Angel looked at him and then, at the TV. I could get use to this shit. He wrapped his arms around her and pulled her close. After a few minutes, they fell asleep.

A buzzing noise woke Angel up. She looked over at the clock on the night stand.

"Fuck!" she hissed, sitting up in the bed.

"You aiight?" Daniel asked, turning over.

"Boy, it's five in the morning. I wasn't tryna spend the night." She stood up, looking for her clothes. "I gotta be to work in a minute."

"Chill, baby." Daniel turned on the light.

"Damn," Angel slid her dress over her head and found her panties on the other side of the room. "So now what?" Angel asked as she put on her shoes and took out her car keys.

Daniel frowned. "What you mean?"

"I mean are we going to continue to talk? See each other?" she asked.

"Yeah of course." He chuckled, pulling her into a hug. "You my boo thing now."

"Oh really?" she kissed him.

"Let that shit stay wet like that," he kissed her on the neck and rubbed her clit through her panties, "and your ass gonna be tied up."

"Humm," she pulled away. "If you say so. I will hit you later." She left.

Chapter Three

Trina and Angel sat at the bar, tossing a few back and talking about their dates. Angel's pussy got wet every time she thought about Daniel. They would be talking on the phone and she would have to put it on mute, so he wouldn't hear her moaning. It was safe to say that he had her ass whipped. It could have been the fact that it had been months since she had some dick, too. Either way, Angel was ready to fuck and suck his ass again.

After being hurt so many times by niggas that claimed they were loyal she was ready to find a man that was going to make her feel like a woman on the inside and out. She wanted to be able to call her dude up to talk about her day and to share intimacy with someone that wasn't out there being for everybody. It didn't seem like a lot to ask but it was damn sure hard to get. Some nights she would stay up crying, feeling insecure about the damage of literal and physical scares of her past. The mirror reminded her of the wounds that covered her skin, but it also reflected the shattered pieces of her heart.

"Damn that nigga got me in a different world." Angel sipped a Long Island Ice Tea.

"Chile, you sound like you in love."

Angel cut her eyes at Trina and said, "Bitch, please."

She told her about the good ass sex they had, and Trina was all ears because her night with Jesse ass was dull as hell. That was two or three hours she would never get back. Shit was good until the motion of the ocean started to sway.

"So how was Jesse?" Angel asked.

"Huh?" Her eyes got big.

"Huh? You heard me."

Trina shrugged her shoulders. "Uhm he was aiight."

"Aiight? That's it?" Angel laughed.

"Yeah, I mean he was decent. It wasn't all that. Not

enough to be bragging about like Daniel."

"Definitely not like Daniel." Angel cracked a smile and slapped her five.

"Shh shh this him calling now. Hey, Jesse what's up?" Trina answered.

"I been thinking about your ass since the other night."

Trina laughs, "Is that right?"

"Hell, yeah shit what's up with you? I'm trying to hook up." He told her.

"Well I'll come through I'll be there in about an hour."

His ass was grinning from ear to ear. "Alright then I'll see you in a minute."

Angel laughed at Trina's expression. "What he talking about?"

"Nothing talking bout he been thinking about a bitch ever since last night." Trina laughed too.

She was okay with going to see him again. Perhaps it would be better, but she was really just trying to run up a check. She would have to sacrifice to get what she felt she deserved. Hell, she would have been happy if the sex was how Angel had described it, but beggars can't be choosers. She had to use what she had to get what she wanted. Damn that just sounded cliché as hell; some straight Player's Club shit. It is what it is though. Everybody wasn't as lucky as Ms. Angel.

"What? Could this be a sign?"

"Girl please! I just put it on him that's all"

"We gone be dating boys. This is fantastic double dates, double weddings and double strollers," Angel joke as she got all excited.

"Slow your roll Lil Miss Impatient. I'm just feeling the nigga out and you all set for us to get married and start a family." Trina rolled her eyes and pulled out her wallet.

She was about to go home and get freshened up before she went to see Jesse. She and Angel left the bar and got into their cars, promising to talk later that day. Angel turned on the radio and blasted a Meek Mills song. She was vibing to the music as she cruised down the main road to her apartment. Things in the neighborhood had surely changed since she was a kid. She could remember when the corner boys wore long V-Neck t-shirts and fitted caps and listened to DMX. She shook her head thinking about the day she and her brother were coming from Max's Liquor Store. Her mother was having a cook out and sent them to get ice and few cases of beers. Angel was getting on Malcom about his tired ass fade and old ass car stereo.

"Lay off, lil sis." He laughed at her corny ass jokes as the turned the corner to their block. A red sports car came flying their way. Malcom tried to swerve but the car smashed right into them at full speed spinning their car several times before it crashed into someone's house. Angel's face hit the dash board as glass and debris flew everywhere.

"Malcom!?" she called for her brother but there was no answer. Her eyes slowly opened, and she realized that he was no longer in the driver's seat of the car.

"Oh my god!" she heard a lady screaming. "My kids! Malcom! Angel!" she yelled.

Angel tried to move her neck, but it hurt too badly. Her mother appeared on the driver's side of the door. She was screaming and pulling on the door, but it wouldn't open.

"What the fuck!" she panted, pulling at the handle. "Get my baby out of there."

Then, first responders arrived and advised her to step to the aside. She cover her face as they cut the top of the car off and pulled Angel from the passenger seat. Tears streamed down her face while they hauled her into the back of an ambulance. "Where is my brother? I need to see my brother!" Angel cried while they tried to access her injuries. Her mother climbed into the ambulance and held her hand.

"Calm down," she stroked the side of her face. "They're

going to help you."

"Malcom? Why aren't you with Malcom?"

Their mother held her breath and said, "I'm sorry. He didn't make it."

Angel burst into tears as the ambulance pulled off. Soon they arrived at the hospital, where Angel learned that both her legs were broke and she had hundreds of small cuts on her neck and arms. Some of them needed stitches and the doctors had to carefully remove the glass particles from her skin.

It was a day she would never forget. There was still a lot of pain there. She missed her brother dearly and often question why she had survived and he didn't. She turned on to her block and parked her car in front of the house.

Angel sat at the breakfast nook in the kitchen, sipping a cup of ice tea. Sometimes she hated being in the house a lone. She missed having someone to talk to or cuddle up with but lately there hasn't been anyone worth her time. As she read a book, the doorbell chimed. She looked at her phone—there were no missed calls or messages. She frowned, wondering who could be at her door unannounced.

"Who?" She asked, looking through the peephole.

"Open this damn door, chile. I gotta piss bad as hell."

Angel laughed, opening the door. "What the hell you doing here?"

Carla burst in and skipped down the hall to the bathroom. She hurried and relieved herself. Angel was sitting at the nook when she walked into the kitchen and opened the refrigerator. She looked around and only saw a pack of sausage and a gallon of milk.

"What you got to eat in here? I'm hungry as hell." She searched the shelves. "You don't go food shopping? Oh, I forgot your ass don't know how to cook." Carla closed the fridge.

Angel grinned and laughed, "You always raiding

someone fridge. And for your info I do know how to cook I just don't."

"And you never going to find a man like that." Carla shook her head.

She found a box of mac and cheese in the cabinet and put it in a bowl with water to cook in the microwave.

Angela sat across from Angel as she waited for it to warm in the microwave. She folded her arms and leaned in real close.

"So, what happened last night."

Angel put the book down in front of her, her eyebrows raising on her forehead and her mouth wide opened, and gasped. "Bitch! Bitch! I ain't never ever have no one fuck me like that."

Carla burst into laughter. The microwave pinged, and she got up saying, "He done snatched your soul?"

"Hell yea!" Angel grinned.

Carla returned to the table, her food drowned in hot sauce. "You spent the night?" she looked at her sister.

"Yeah, kinda." Angel shrugged her shoulders.

She remembered the good sex she had with Daniel and her insides were burning, she wanted to tell Carla to leave so that she could call him over, but she sat there and gave her details.

"Oh, my goodness. I can't believe you slept over there!" Carla shook her head. "And why you have sex with him on the first night? I done told you that you never going to find love like that."

"Girl! Shut the hell up! Don't try and act like you're so holier than thou like you ain't a freak." Angel shot her a dirty look. "You over here acting like you never got down on the first night. I recall you fucking a few dudes whose names you didn't even know."

Carla was one of those friends that liked to pretend that she had a whole lot of dignity and she always could read someone else. She could tell you all your problems and try to solve them. You would never hear Carla's problems though. She was private, never really wanted anyone to know that deep down inside she's a hoe.

"That was before I was married." She shoved food in her mouth.

"Uhm if my memory serves me correct Derrick was after the fact." Angel corrected.

Carla spit out her food and swatted Angel's hand. "Angel?"

Angel frowned and hit her back, "What? You ain't finna sit in my house and make me feel cheap."

"You promised not to bring that up." Carla huffed, knowing that she should not be judging.

"Hell, I ain't married, yet. I'ma enjoy my freedom." Angel shrugged, rolling her eyes.

Carla continued to stuff her face, but Angel was preparing herself for all the bullshit she was about to say. This was nothing new. Carla believed that since God blessed her with a husband everyone was supposed to be out there looking for everlasting love. Now days, that shit just didn't exist though. Don't get it twisted, there are some good men out there but half of them were already taken. Besides, people weren't rushing to get married. Angel wasn't a fool. She wasn't trying to move in with him, she was simply having a good time.

"Damn, well just don't move too fast." Carla warned. "You know how you get." She carried her bowl to the sink.

Carla was trying to make sure Angel wasn't going to get hurt again. They'd been friends long enough for her to be honest. Angel, sometimes, let those scars rule her heart. She thought that she deserved a lot of the mess others put on her. she was getting ready to give her a piece of her mind when she heard Angel on the phone. She must be talking to him, Carla watched her blush and swirl around in her seat.

"Miss Angel, what's good?" Daniel asked on the phone

"Hey Daniel, nothing much hanging with my girl."

"Okay I see you busy hit me later."

"Uh uh you're not getting away that easy. Were you trying to see me?"

She smiled, knowing that he would say yes. She was glad she had given him a second chance after he dipped out on their initial date. She got up and walked down the hall to her bedroom as she waited to hear what plan Daniel had.

"That all depends on you. If you can get away." He said, slyly.

"How fast you need me?" She grinned.

"Be on your way." Daniel demanded, his dick already swollen in his lap.

"I'm on it." She hung up the phone and backtracked into the kitchen. "Okay Carla I enjoyed our little conversation but you gotta go!"

Carla was already putting her phone in her purse and taking out her car keys. This seemed to be a normality in their friendship. Angel was always quick to be on beck and call for some dick. I hope that shit worth it, Carla thought.

"Humph, that nigga got you wrapped up already." She shook her head, heading for the front door.

"Nah," Angel rolled her eyes, "I got his ass sprung."

"Alright go ahead," Carla opened the door and turned to kiss Angel on the cheek, "but remember what I said."

"I will, Mother. Talk to you later.

Chapter Four

Daniel came into the apartment and took a seat on the couch. Angel was in the kitchen whipping up a quick meal. She knew her baby was probably hungry after chilling all day with his boys. She was smiling from ear to ear because she loved spending time with him. She went into the living room and handed him a beer. She took a big sniff and she inhaled she got this strange feeling.

"You said you were out with the fellas, right?" she looked over at him as he took a sip.

Daniel watched her for a minute and replied, "Yeah why you looking at me like that?"

"Like what?" She cut her eyes at him.

He was starting to feel a bit uncomfortable and his heart was pounding. He knew he should have taken his ass home before coming over there. "Like I'm in trouble or something."

"That fragrance, I smelled it before." She leaned closer to him. "And you said you were out with your boys?"

"Fragrance? What fragrance?" Daniel acted like he was confused, sniffing himself.

"The one that's in your clothes."

"Baby didn't I tell you?" he touched the side of her face. "You have nothing to be jealous about."

"This has nothing to do with me being jealous." Angel shook her head. "I know what I smell."

"The fuck you think you smell? Fuck you is? A hound dog?"

"It smell like that bottle of perfume I found in your cabinet."

"So, you was going through my shit?" Daniel stood up. "There you go tripping again."

"It's always me huh?" Angel stood up too.

"You don't see me starting shit or accusing you of shit, do you?" he grabbed her by the arm.

Angel snatched away. "Cause you can't. Cause I don't give you a reason to."

"And neither do I," He snapped as she puts her hand on her hip. "Alright once and I apologize since then. What else you want me to do?"

Angel pushed pass him and walked toward the kitchen. "If we're going to be together I'm gone need to be able to trust you"

"Oh, so now you don't trust me?" Daniel followed her.

"No, I'm not saying that." She shook her head. "You either seeing some bitch or you like bitch perfume."

"Oh, so now you calling me a fag, huh?" He grabbed her by the back of the neck.

Angel braced herself against the stove. "You're twisting my words. Let me go."

"Okay so again you don't trust me? That's a yes or no question." He squeezed tighter.

"Yes, but…"

"No buts either you do, or you don't cause honestly I can't be playing these childish ass games with you." He shouted.

"What?" Angel winced.

"Angel I like you in fact I like you a lot, but my last relationship was full of games that's why I left her. And I thought you were different." He mushed her and released her neck.

"I am. I am different baby" Angel turned around as she trying to convince him. "Please don't go please don't leave me. I'm sorry." She wiped away tears.

"Come here," He put his arms around her. "You got to trust me. I'm not going to hurt you I told you before you got me now whether or not you keep me it's up to you."

He lifted her head up to kiss her then they went into her bedroom. Daniel undressed her. She was an emotional wreck which made her hornier than usual. She was more aggressive in bed this time maybe the thought of losing him made her want to please him, want to show him what he would miss out on if he left her.

"Oh, baby I trust you! I trust you! I trust you!" She screamed out as she bounced up and down on his dick until he came.

"That's what I'm talking about. I ain't going nowhere."

They just laid there in each other's arms. By morning Daniel had gotten up taken a shower and left. Angel woke up and rolled over to empty bed.

"Psst," she sucked through her teeth. "I wanted him to still be here. Oh well." She signed as she rolled back over and went back to sleep but was woke up by the knocking on her door. She looked through the peephole and opened the door.

"Get up, get up, get up, rise and shine. Wipe that sleep out your eyes." Trina sang.

"What are you doing here so early?" Angel yawned.

"Early? Girl it's three in the afternoon get your lazy ass up like you had to work last night."

"I did," Angel smirked as she rolled her eyes."

"Ooh you nasty. Bitch tell me all about it."

"Ain't nothing to tell he came over we talked, had sex. I woke up he was gone."

"Oh, don't worry bout that y'all way past one-night stands. So, you ain't gotta worry about him hitting it and quitting it he'll be back. But on another note your boy called and asked me to come out with him tonight."

"You going?"

"I don't know. I'm thinking about it." Trina told her as she looked the refrigerator for something to eat. "Damn Bitch hurry up and get dressed so we can go to a restaurant or something to eat. Hell, that's probably why he left your ass this morning his ass was hungry." She burst into laughter.

"Shut up I'll be right back." Angel laughed as she heads to get ready.

Later on, that evening while Trina was out with Jesse she called up Angel to see what she was doing.

"Hello?" Angel answered

"What you doing?"

"Hello?" Angel pressed the phone up against her ear. The noisy background made it hard to hear.

"Hold on," Trina said as she made her way to the bathroom. "I said what you doing?"

"Okay now I can hear you nothing watching TV." Angel told her

"Well why don't you come out and have some fun?"

"Naw I'm waiting on Daniel to call me back, so I can see if he wants to hook up."

"Daniel? You want me to ask him? He's somewhere in here." Trina affirmed.

Angel rolled her eyes because she had been trying to get in touch with him to no avail. She snapped her teeth and waited for Trina to come back to the phone.

"Probably cause it's so many thots in here he can't see straight." Trina chuckled. "Hell, I don't even see his ass nowhere.

"Well I trust him so naw you gone head and enjoy yourself. I'm just going to sit this one out. Tell Jesse I said what up.'

"Alright, but don't be expecting no full report tomorrow."

"I won't, talk to you later." Angel hung up. "I can't believe he's not answering his phone or calling me back? He's probably all up in there in one of them bitches face grinning while I'm at home bored. I should get dressed and go out there. Matter of fact I am." Angel decided as she got up and dressed and called Trina to let her know.

She looked at herself in the mirror. Her ass was sitting

up high in a short low-cut dress. She smiled and grabbed her purse. This boy really got me fucked up, Angel thought as she climbed into her car. She turned up Cardi B's "Drip" as she pushed the pedal to the metal. The parking lot was filled with cars and a few thugs, you know the ones that dress in True Religion Jeans, Timberlands, and white tees. They were drinking from red cups and puffing on blunts. Trina was standing out front with a cigarette to her lips when Angel approached the front door.

"What's good, boo?" Trina asked, surprised to see her. "I thought you were staying home."

"Okay, where is he?" Angel put her hands on her hips.

"Who? Daniel. Chile please. I thought you trusted him." Trina was clearly drunk. "Last time I seen him he was dancing with some chick."

"Yeah? Okay we'll see about that." Angel whipped open the door with her money and ID in her hand.

Her eyes quickly scanned the room. Daniel had his arms wrapped around some hoochie on the other end of the dance floor. Angel bit her bottom lip and started toward them.

"Angel!" Trina called behind her. "What you bout to do?"

"See what's up with my man."

"Look at me and let me know if you bout to be in here scrapping."

"Naw girl I'm bout to be on my best behavior watch," Angel grinned as she walked through the crown and over to the booth Daniel was sitting in. When he made eye contact her, he stood up coolly.

"Hey baby, what are you doing here?" He tried to reach for a hug.

"Don't 'hey baby' me. Who this?" Angel stared at the girl. "This one of the fellas."

"Nah, Angel, chill. We just kicking it." Daniel tried to

tell her.

"Kicking it my ass. Look like you up in here with some bitch."

"Watch ya mouth." The girl rolled her eyes.

"Nah, bitch, you need to go find your own nigga and leave mine alone."

"Who the fuck is you? Nivea?"

Angel laughed and took a deep breath. Then she backed up and smacked Daniel. He must have really lost his mind to be up in the club with her friend there while he was with some other chick. She rolled her eyes and stomped away. She went back to the bar and ordered a drink. Daniel sat back down at the table, staring at her.

"Everything good?" Trina asked, raising a glass to her lips as Angel sipped hers.

"Yup." Angel looked over her shoulder.

"Okay cause when ole girl stood up I thought we was gonna have to whoop her ass." Trina laughed.

"Naw it's cool I handled it. Like I said I trust him, but that don't mean I ain't watching. Let's go dance I ain't letting that shit get to me." Angel pulled Trina by the arm.

"Well you a bigger person than me cause I would have fucked them both up."

Angel was swaying her hips back and forth, dancing to the beat. She put a little extra into it because she knew that Daniel was watching. He was sitting there looking like a lost puppy while she shook her ass on the dance floor. Suddenly, he was standing behind her.

"Come on," he grabbed her by the arms. "Let's go."

"I ain't ready to go." Angel pulled away.

He snatched her arm again and pulled her close to him. His lips were touching her ear and he was breathing heavily. He smelled as if he had been drinking all night. Angel curled up her bottom lip and tried to pull away again.

"Trust me, you don't want your friends to know what I

have in store for you." He whispered.

"Is that supposed to be a threat?" she asked.

He squeezed her arm tighter and pulled her toward the door. "You got too much mouth." He pushed her out the door.

"Let me go!" Angel pushed him back.

"Man, get your ass in the car." He shoved her.

Angel folded her arms across her chest as he slammed the passenger door closed. Daniel walked around the car and got into the driver's seat. He reached over the console and grabbed her by the neck.

"So, who was she?" Angel shouted.

"Angel?" Daniel squinted his eyes, "Why you always got to play so much? I be seeing these other bitches but they ain't you."

Angel could feel the anger radiating off him and the look in his eyes reminded her of the look her father would give her mother. She closed her eyes and took a deep breath.

"Calm down and get your hands off me."

"So, you a man now? You think you can beat me?" he screamed in her face.

"You out here fucking these bitches but I'm the one you hurting? You said you love me." Angel cried.

Daniel slowly let her go and started the car engine. Angel rubbed her hands around her neck and caught her breath. He definitely wasn't the man she had met. She stared out the window as they drove to his apartment. He parked the car.

"How am I supposed to get my car?" she asked.

"I'll take you to get it in the morning." Daniel opened his door. "Now get your ass in here and take off that little ass dress." He barked.

Angel pulled herself together and climbed out of the car. She wanted to just call an Uber and get the hell out of there. She knew that would piss him off even more, so she followed Daniel into the house. She took off her shoes at the door and slid into the bathroom and closed the door. She peeled the dress off and folded it, placing it on the back of the toilet seat. When she came out the bathroom Daniel was sitting on the edge of the bed in his boxers.

"Daniel?" Angel asked, rolling her eyes "Who was she?"

"Nobody." He repeated.

"What was y'all talking about?" she wanted to know.

"Nothing." He shrugged, picking up the remote.

"It sure in the hell didn't look like you and nobody was talking about nothing. It look like y'all was on a date." Angel laid back on the bed.

"Get the fuck out of here." Daniel huffed. "What date?"

"Y'all was all tucked away in the corner all romantic and shit."

"Man, you trippin." He waved his hand.

"See that's just it I'm always trippin and you never wrong. It's always me. But I know what I saw. You feeling all on that bitch titties but I'm trippin."

"Man, you gone believe what you want to believe. I done told you what it was I mean like I said you either trust me or you don't. I'm about to go take a shower."

"Yeah go ahead and wash your nasty trick off," She flipped him the bird. As soon as she heard the water running in the bathroom she decided to snoop. She went to the bathroom and slid his phone out his pocket then went to the bedroom. She started going through his call log and scrolling through the most recent ones which was right before she got there.

"Ain't this a bitch! That lying mutha'fucka. I can't believe you had the audacity to switch it up on me." As she started crying just then Daniel walked in the room wearing a towel holding his clothes in his hand. Looking around the room when she holds his phone up.

"Looking for this?" she waved it in his face.

"Yeah I thought I dropped it in the car." Daniel reached for it.

"Naw it was right here," She hissed as she handed to him. "Can I ask you a question?'

"Of course."

"Who is Erica?" he looked shocked wondering could he have been so careless and forgot to put the lock back on his phone.

"A friend why?" He answered nonchalantly.

Angel folded her arms across her chest and bit her bottom lip. "Cause I'm wondering why you asked her to come over this late?"

"Aww it wasn't nothing." He waved his hand.

"Then please tell me what it's like cause the way I see it you're a hoe."

"Watch your mouth!"

"What? You mad at the truth? Come on now you got Erica, Sabrina and Keisha all as the last time convos you had before me. What's up with that?"

"Ain't shit up with that. I ain't gotta explain shit we ain't married."

"Oh, you think so?" Angel asked as she jumped up. "You feel you ain't gotta explain shit cause we ain't married? I'm your girlfriend what does that count for?"

"Nothing." Daniel told her

"You son of a bitch!"

Then out of nowhere Daniel cocked his hand back and slapped the shit out of Angel.

"Mutha'fucka you hit me?" Angel screeched as she lunges towards him and he threw her against the bed so hard and forceful that she fell over on the floor. As she stumbles to get up Daniel noticed the blood coming from her lip.

"I'm sorry Angel. I'm so sorry." Daniel reached out to her.

"Don't touch me Daniel! Don't ever touch me." Angel

cried as she pulled away.

"Baby I'm so sorry. I shouldn't have pushed you it all happened so fast. I don't know what happened."

"Look at my face Daniel!" Angel looked in the mirror as she started crying uncontrollably. He went and got some ice for her face. When he comes back in the room she's in the mirror crying and shaking her head.

"Baby I'm sorry. I just want you to understand that you can't be talking to me any kind of way. You know that ticks me off." I will make this up to you. You name it I'll do it cause I love you".

"You love me?" Angel sniffled as she lifted up her head.

"Of course, I love you and you're my baby and I want to keep it that way." He spoke softly, pulling her into his arms, looking at the busted lip he gave her. "I just don't want people judging me".

"They won't cause they won't know especially my friends." she started to clean it with a towel.

"You would do that for me? You will cover up my fuck ups?" Daniel looked down at her with a smile.

"Of course, baby. If anyone asks I'll just say I fell and hit my face or something." Angel sighed.

"That's why I love you cause you got me like I got you." He kissed her.

The next morning Angel woke up with a throbbing headache she looked around for Daniel but didn't see him. She got up out the bed and looked in the mirror. She had a bruise on her left cheek and her lip was busted.

"Ha-ha girl you know I'm clumsy as hell. I fell out the bed hit my face and bit my tongue in the process." Angel rehearsed her lines.

There was no way she was ever going to admit that Daniel hit her. She would lie and cover it up as best she could. She deserved it, didn't she? She got all in his face, went through his phone. She wanted to get her ass beat and he gave it to her. Right? She looked at her face in the mirror and covered the bruise with make-up.

"Morning baby." Daniel said as she turned towards the door.

"Hey." She smiled, shyly.

"How you feeling?"

"I got a really bad headache."

"I brought you some Tylenol for that and some orange juice."

"Thank you" She reached out as he handed them to her. "I keep trying to go over my story so it's convincing and believable."

"I feel so bad I swear I do."

"I know you do. I know you ain't mean it."

"Naw. Hell naw. I don't know what came over me. I've never done that before and I never will again." "You promise?"

"I promise baby," Daniel pulled her into his arms as he started kissing all over her body.

Then her phone started ringing she went over to the nightstand and answered it.

"Hey, you good?" Trina asked. "You left your car at the club and…"

"Yea, I'm good," She looked over her shoulder at Daniel who sucked his teeth, "but I can't talk right now."

"You okay?" she asked.

"Uh, yeah," Angel brushed her hand over her head. "I'm fine. I will call you later." She hung up.

Daniel pulled her down on the bed. He kissed her on the neck and sniffed her hair. He was touching all over her body like the first time they made love. She was tense, nervous and scared.

Chapter Five

Angel was curled up in Daniel's bed, holding her stomach. She thought she could sit up but as soon as she did, vomit spilled from her mouth. She got the strength to pick up the phone and call Trina.

"Hello?" She answered, feeling the urge to throw up again. "Do me a favor, Trina."

"What? Girl I'm with my man." She snapped.

"Please. Go get me a pregnancy test."

Trina was there for the drama, so she rolled from underneath Jesse and went to the store when she arrived at Daniel's apartment she was lying in the middle of the bed with a bag. She leaned over and threw up.

"Eww. Here bitch hurry up and piss on this." She handed her the bag.

Angel drug herself out of the bed and went into the bathroom. The test was positive, so she called Daniel. For that news, he hurried home.

"You sure," he asked holding her face.

"Yes," Angel smiled.

"Angel I'm so exciting I'm gone be an auntie. Ooh I got to call Carla."

When Trina walked in the living room Angel pulled Daniel to the side, wrapping her arms around his waist. He looked down at her and kissed her on the lips.

"How you feel about it? Cause I won't have it if you don't want me to." Angel told him.

Later on, that night Angel called Daniel's phone, but it kept going to voicemail. She sent him a text and he instantly replied. All she wanted was a bottle of Ginger Ale and to lay in his arms all night. She wanted to kiss and hold on to him. They were having a baby together and she wanted to make sure that he was going to love her and their baby no matter what. She knew that he was flirtatious, always in some bitch face but if she kept him happy she wouldn't have to worry about any of that. All she had to do was play her role.

"Can't talk now."

Angel frowned, knowing that wasn't how he normally was with her. She tossed the phone on the bed and went into the kitchen. There had to be something in there to settle her stomach. She found a can of coke and went back to bed, to check her phone. He hadn't replied or called her back. After a few minutes the phone rang.

"Hello."

"Yeah what's up?"

"Where are you? And why are you whispering?" Angel frowned.

Daniel snapped his teeth. "I'll be there in a minute."

"I thought we were gone celebrate."

"We are we are calm down."

"Can you bring some food when you come?"

"Yeah I got you. Now I gotta go see you in a bit."

Before she could say bye, he hung up. It was way after two in the morning when Daniel got home. He was stumbling and knocking stuff over because he was drunk. He came in the house and tried to creep passed the room and into the bathroom. Angel got up and turned on the light.

"Well I'm glad I wasn't waiting on you to get here to eat." She stood there with her hands on her hips.

"My bad Angel I got caught up."

"You got caught up? It took you four hours to finally decide to come home?" she snapped her teeth.

"Naw I told you I got caught up," he yelled as he started getting angry.

"Were you with another bitch?"

Daniel sucked his teeth. "Naw I wasn't with another bitch."

"Let me smell your dick." She grabbed at his belt.

"What?" he pushed her hand away.

"You heard me. Let me smell your dick."

"Man watch out," Daniel brushed pass as he pushed her out the way.

"Cause you know you lying. Got me pregnant sitting up in your house waiting on you. I could have been at my own shit for all this." Angel followed him into the bedroom.

"You trippin."

"There go that word again you forever saying it's me. I don't know why I keep putting myself in this situation with you. You can't even be honest with me." She started to cry.

"You want me to be honest? Yes, I was with a female tonight and you know what? It felt good not being nagged all night." He admitted.

Angel couldn't believe what she was hearing. Here it was one of the happiest days of her life and it was turning out to be one of the worse.

"Oh my God I can't believe you just said that to me," Angel snapped as she started crying and getting louder. "After everything I've done to make you happy this is my thanks?"

"Oh, here you go with that bullshit man damn." Daniel snarled as he took off his pants. "I'm a man. I am going to do whatever the fuck I wanna do. Take that shit or leave it. All you do is nag nag nag."

"Man fuck you. Me and my baby going to be good, with or without you." She slipped on her pants.

"Fuck," She realized she didn't have her car. She pulled out her phone to order an Uber.

"Fuck you think you going? You ain't going nowhere with my baby in your stomach."

"I'm getting the fuck out of here Daniel. I don't need you." Angel cried, trying to type her address into the phone.

"Man…" He snatched the phone from her hand and tossed it across the room, shattering it on the wall.

"Daniel!" she yelled, trying to run from him.

He grabbed her hair and pulled her down to the ground. She was kicking and screaming as he kicked her in the stomach.

"Please, Daniel. What about the baby?"

"Shut the fuck up!" he screamed. "You think you going to leave me? You don't do shit without me telling you, you hear me? Huh, bitch?" he punched her.

Angel laid there, curled up and holding her stomach. She was trying desperately to protect her baby. He kept kicking her and when he was done, he pulled her onto the bed and grabbed her by the face.

"Look at me, if you ever try and leave me again I'll kill you," he threatened as she laid there crying all out of breath. "Do you hear me?"

"Yes, I hear you," Angel whispered as she laid there crying in pain. Daniel walked out of the room and went to take a shower. Angel just laid there and didn't move she was scared for her life and of her unborn child. About ten minutes goes by before Daniel came back into the room. He walked over to the bed and leaned over her. Then, he reached his arms out to her. Angel flinched back as if she was trying to block from getting hit.

"Come on baby get up and clean yourself up." He whispered

"Please don't touch me." Angel cried.

"Angel let me help you." He reached for her again. "You getting blood on my sheets.

"I can do it," Angel winced as she tried to get up. One hand on her stomach the other on the side of the bed.

"Baby, I'm sorry." He tried to tell her.

"That's what you said last time," Angel looked away.

"But I mean it this time," Daniel said as he put his arm around her and pulled her closer. "I think the thought of losing you puts me in a place. I don't even know what comes over me."

Angel sat there rocking back and forth from the pain

holding her stomach.

"I don't know who you are anymore."

"It's still me." He ran his fingers through her hair. Angel flinched again then let out a loud sigh.

"You don't have to be afraid of me. I'm not gone hurt you."

She wanted to believe him, but he had said that to her before. She got up and went into the bathroom and started to clean herself up. Tears were still pouring down her cheeks and her stomach was hurting. She laid down in the bed next to him and tried to sleep but she was in a lot of pain.

"Oh my God! Daniel wake up," Angel panicked as she shook his arm.

"What? What are you screaming for?"

"I think it's the baby," She moved the covers back.

"Oh shit," he jumped up. "Let me help you up out the bed. Come on I gotta get you to the hospital."

He helped her get changed and dressed so they could go. When they arrived at the hospital Daniel ran in and got a wheelchair to take her in. Acting as if he was a concerned father of the child and loving man to Angel. He held her hand the whole time that she was there from beginning to end. After being there for a couple hours Angel learned that she had a miscarriage she broke down crying hysterically. Staring at Daniel she couldn't believe that he had taken her precious baby's life because he couldn't control his temper. The nurse handed her some Kleenex as the doctor was going into details about the procedure she would have to have. Daniel started rubbing her back trying to console her as she was steady breaking down. As he looked into her eyes a tear fell from his eye. "I'm so sorry baby" as he laid his head in her lap. Not knowing whether to believe his apology or not considering he was just the cause of her losing her baby. She just sat there frozen. Over the next couple days Angel distanced herself from everybody including Daniel. She had left his house and went home with no intentions on going back. The hurt and pain she was feeling was unbearable she just wanted to be by herself for a few days and needed space. She finally reached out to her girls and asked if they could come through.

"I got here as fast as I could. Are you alright?"

"No. No Carla I'm not" Angel looked at her as she broke down. Trina went and grabbed her some tissue.

"Is it the baby?" she asked.

"There is no baby," She sobbed, grabbing the tissue from Trina and blowing her nose.

"Wait! What do you mean there's no baby?"

"I had a miscarriage."

"I'm so sorry Angel," Trina said as they both gave her a hug.

"Is there anything we can do for you?"

"No."

"How did Daniel take it?" Trina asked.

Angel looked at her and rolled her eyes. Then just put her head down and sighed.

"What's wrong? Talk to us."

"Daniel is the reason I lost my baby."

"Hold the fuck up," Trina jumped up pointing her finger at Angel. "What the fuck you mean he made you lose your baby?"

"Last week we argued about him texting back and forth with some bitches and one thing led to another."

"And?"

"Did he hit you?"

"Yes" Carla and Trina sucked through their teeth and rolled her eyes. "He hit me, he punched me, kicked me and pushed me."

"I'm so sorry you had to go through that."

"Me too."

"Thanks y'all. I mean I don't know what I did wrong."

"What you did wrong?" Carla asked as Trina got upset.

"You ain't do shit wrong. That mother sucka had no business putting his goddamn hands on you."

"Trina's right he had no business putting his hands on you. Did you make a police report?"

"Naw I didn't," as she said back on the couch.

"Why not?"

"Cause Trina I didn't want the police all up in my business that's why."

Trina shook her head.

"Angel it's not so much them being in your business. It's to make a report so you have it on record. Suppose he do it again?"

"He won't."

"And how do you know?"

"Cause he told me he wouldn't do it again and I believe him this time."

"Wait. So, he hit you before? Angel got quiet and started tapping her foot. "Well I just be damn. He did, didn't he?"

"Yes," Angel admitted Trina threw her hands up.

"Now what the fuck Angel we're supposed to be your homegirls."

"Y'all are my girls."

"Well how come you didn't tell us then?" Carla interrupted a tear fell down Angel's face.

"Do you know how embarrassed I was? Hiding a busted lip from y'all. Staying over Daniel's so I could heal and no one seeing the bruises on my body."

"My God."

"Angel we're so sorry. I can't imagine what you went through, but you can't let him get away with this."

"Trina's right Angel he has to be held accountable for what he's done."

"I said no!" Then, she got up and paced the floor. "I'm not making a police report end of discussion. Now can we just go grab something to eat or something? I just want to get some air."

"Of course, let's go," Trina said as they headed out.

Chapter Six

Damn, Angel rolled over in Daniel's bed. He was still snoring, so she grabbed the remote and turned on the TV. It had been six months since she lost the baby and she was still trying to get over it. She never got a chance to hear its heartbeat or to know if it was a boy or girl, but she still loved it. It would have been her baby and by now she was supposed to have it in her arms. She tried not to think too much about it but as she laid across from Daniel, her emotions were overcoming her. Before the tears started to fall she turned over on her side and took a few deep breaths. She reached over and picked up her phone while searching for something good to watch. There was a missed call and message from Carla. As usual she was being nosey and asking when they could all hang out. Angel started a group message with her and Trina, so they could plan something. She longed for a day with her girls because lately Daniel was the only other person she chopped it up with. She was wondering what was going on with her friends and she needed a drink.

"What you doing, baby?" Daniel asked, sitting up in the bed.

"Watching TV and chopping it up with my girls." She told him.

"Nah," he reached for the phone. "Who you talking to at two in the morning?"

Angel cut her eyes at him, "You ain't bout to go through my phone." She held it away from him.

He climbed over her and reached for the phone again. When Angel refused to give him the phone he pinned her down on the bed and squeezed her wrist until she let it go.

"Daniel," She huffed. "Is it that fucking serious??"

"Must be you trying to hide shit." He sat on the edge of the bed and hurriedly read through her messages. He was grunting and mumbling stuff under his breath while she tried to grab it.

"Ain't nothing on there." She told him, constantly but he was determined to find something.

"Yo…" he said. "I'ma need you to go change ya number. I'm deleting Facebook and IG."

Angel frowned and snatched the phone out of his hands. "Man, go head…"

"Go head?" he jumped up. "Get the fuck out."

Angel couldn't believe her fucking ears, but he wasn't going to kick her out twice. She jumped up her feet and grabbed her pants off the back of the chair. He was standing there with his hands on his hips. She glared at him but didn't say anything. She snatched her keys off the dresser and put on her shoes. Who the fuck this nigga think he is? She hopped in her car and sped off.

"What up freak? I ain't heard from you in a couple days." Carla answered the phone.

Angel was trying to hide her tears, "Yo, he told me to get out."

"What?" Carla sat up in bed. "Out? At this time of the morning. I thought he was over there giving you the good, good." Carla laughed.

There was silence on the phone.

"Angel?" Carla finally said, "Are you okay?"

"No," Angel shuttered. "I'm on my way to my apartment. I'm not even sure how I feel right now. This the first time he ever acted like this." She pulled into a parking space.

"I'm on my way." Carla hung up.

Angel gathered herself and went in to the house. She pulled out a bottle of wine and sat at the table. She replayed the scene in her head. Maybe he was going through something, she thought. She had been through worse in her previous relationships, but Daniel was different. Maybe it was a little foolish of her to fight with him over the phone because she doesn't have anything to hide. But on the other hand, it's a matter of privacy. She would never go through his phone and she thought he would have the same respect for her. while she waited for Carla to arrive, her phone rang. It was Daniel, but she didn't answer. He called back several more times, leaving a few voicemails. Then, he sent her thirty text messages.

Fuck! Angel tossed the phone on the counter. The doorbell rang, and she rushed to answer it. To her surprise, it was not Carla but Daniel.

"What are you doing here?"

"Come on home." He reached to hug her. "I'm sorry."

Angel wiped her tears, backing up into the apartment. "But Daniel…"

"Look baby. I won't ever do that again. I freaked out. I think I…look, I love you, girl and I don't wanna lose you." He touched her chin.

"You love me?" she asked, trying to resist a smile.

"Yeah," he hugged her and kissed her on the head.

Angel reached up, wrapping her arms around his neck. He kissed her on the lips and she kissed him back.

"The fuck?" Carla screeched. "Get away from her."

"Carla…"

"No, he gotta go." She waved her hand in his direction.

"It's okay." Angel told her. "We made up."

Carla sighed giving him the side eye. She went into the kitchen and looked around. She wanted to tell Angel that he wasn't worth it. People have problems in their relationships all the time, though. She wasn't going to interfere, yet. After Angel assured her that everything was okay, she left.

Daniel sat on the couch and turned on the TV. Angel grabbed the bottle of wine and sat down next to him.

"Don't let that happen again." She poured a glass.

"I won't baby." He pulled her feet into his lap.

She rolled her eyes and sipped her drink. She leaned back on the couch and tried to forget about what happened. It wasn't the first time a man had gotten out of pocket with her, but she prayed he would stick to his word.

"I'm going to bed." She put the glass on the table and went upstairs.

She laid her pants on the back of the chase and pulled back her sheets. In the back of her mind she was praying that Daniel would catch the hint. Her pussy was a little moist and the arguing just made her hornier. She laid there, heart pounding, listening for his footsteps. Finally, he stepped into the room as naked as the day he was born. His hardened dick was slinging from side to side as he approached the side of the bed. He pressed the tip of it against her lips and she opened her mouth as wide as she could. He pushed the back of her head until his entire shaft was engulfed by her mouth.

"Damn baby." He rubbed her leg as she sucked his dick. Then, he spread them apart and slid his finger into her pussy.

She couldn't take it anymore, so she got on all fours and let him push his uncovered dick into her wet pussy. She was moaning and groaning underneath him. Was it the power of the dick or did she really believe that he was sorry? That didn't matter she got her rocks off and fell asleep wrapped in his arms.

The next day she had her number changed, like he asked, and deleted her social media accounts. She didn't want to lose her good thing. She was starting to fall for Daniel and nothing was going to stop him from loving her.

After texting Carla and Trina her new number she went home and started to clean the house. She thought about all the time she was spending with Daniel. Even if she moved in with him she would keep her apartment. She learned a long time ago not to put all her eggs in one basket.

The phone rang and both Carla and Trina were on the line.

"Chile, I'm mad you let that nigga talk you in to changing your number." Carla said.

"Right," Trina agreed, "he must have magic dick or something."

Angel walked around her apartment, listening to Carla and Trina go on and on about how toxic this relationship could be. She knew that Daniel was tripping a little bit, but she didn't care.

"Y'all are wrong about him." She shook her head.

Trina snapped her teeth. "We're not and you know it but all I'ma say about it is be careful."

"Yeah, we got your back." Carla added.

Angel sat on the edge of her bed and sighed. "I know ya'll tryna look out and I love ya'll for that." She smiled. "Oh yeah. Daniel had asked me to chill with him in Vegas this weekend." She changed the subject.

"Vegas? So, he tryna play make up?" Carla asked.

"I guess and I'ma let him. Hell, I need a vacay."

"A free one? Hell yeah, I would take that shit too." Trina laughed.

Carla thought it was a bad idea, but she kept it to herself. She knew that Angel wouldn't listen anyway. All she could do was hope that Daniel wouldn't hurt her. As a counselor, it was hard for her not to judge people and make assumptions based on their actions. Carla couldn't help but to think that Daniel was a womanizer.

"Well enjoy yourself and we'll see you when you get back." Trina said.

"Oh, yeah I'ma be shaking this ass all over the place." Angel exclaimed.

Carla butted in, "Don't let Daniel hear you say that shit."

"Carla would you cut it out?" Angel asked. "He said he was sorry. Now, if he wanna spend his monies on me I will let him."

"Ain't nothing free. Never forget that. Girls, I gotta go. I will hit ya'll later.'" Carla hung up.

She wasn't about to sit there and listen to Angel go on and on about a nigga that made her change her number and delete her accounts.

Trina snapped her teeth, "That bitch always got her panties in a bunch."

"She means well." Angel chuckled. "Anyway, let me call him and see what time I need to be ready."

They hung up.

Chapter Seven

Angel pulled her suitcase from the trunk of the Uber and looked around. Daniel said that he was already at the airport and that he would meet her outside, but she didn't see him anywhere. She took out her phone and called him.

"Where are you?" she looked around again.

"Over here," he said, hastily.

"Over where, Daniel?"

"By Gate-28."

Angel looked up to see where she was. She was standing in front of Gate-28 and his ass was not there. She snapped her teeth and walked toward the door. She was getting ready to give him a mouthful when she spotted him.

"I thought you were going to meet me outside, got me out there looking crazy." She rolled her eyes.

"I said I was going to meet you at the entrance of the gate."

"Whatever." She sorted through her purse for her ID. "We need to check our stuff in."

Daniel took her suitcase and pulled her hand into his.

Angel was so excited not only to be going to Las Vegas but with her man. She was smiling from ear-to-ear sitting next to him.

"You gone be sleep in a minute." He looked over at her. "I thought you were staying woke?"

Shaking her head, Angel replied, "Nope I'm just relaxing; enjoying this flight with my man."

"Oh, is that right?" He smirked.

"Yes, sir." She nodded as he leaned over to kiss her on her head.

The hotel was beautiful, high ceilings and art work. Angel and Daniel retreated to their room to get ready for Vegas Night Life. He went into the bathroom and turned on the shower. A few minutes later, Angel slipped in behind him. She washed his back, kissing him here and there. He continued to groom himself while she washed her hair.

Daniel was looking as fresh as he did the day they met, draped in a back Coogi sweater, True Religion jeans and tall cans. Angel was wrapped in a tight mini dress and a pair of black heels. He admired her from the bed, knowing that he was going to fuck her brains out when they returned to the room. She applied a light layer of makeup and lip gloss to her lips.

"Damn," Daniel licked his lips.

"What?"

"I think I got the finest woman in Vegas."

Angel laughed and sat on his lap, kissing him on the cheek. "Is that so?"

"Hell yeah," he squeezed her butt. "You fine as hell!"

The club was lit. There was ass shaking everywhere, clouds of loud in the air and the music was jumping. Angel leaned over the bar, throwing back another shot of Mango Ciroc. She looked around the crowded area, searching for Daniel's face. Fuck, she fixed her eyes on him as he smiled in some bitch's face. This nigga really got me fucked up. The white liquor had her a little gassed up and she was not about to tolerate her man whispering in some hoe's ear. She stumbled over to them, her hand on her hip.

"Daniel?" he pushed his shoulder.

He looked at her with bewilderment and took a step back. "Oh, I know damn well you ain't just put your damn hands on me." He snarled.

"And I know you ain't over here in some hoe face."

"Hoe?" the girl snapped her neck. "Who the fuck you calling a hoe?"

Angel rolled her eyes and snapped her teeth. "Bitch you better get on."

Daniel snatched Angel by the arm and pulled her away. He was gritting his teeth and mumbling something under his breath. Angel was A-1 hot, mad as hell that he would even think it was okay to disrespect her like this. When they were outside of the club, he pushed her against the wall and wrapped one hand around her neck.

"The fuck wrong with you?" he asked.

"Get yo hands off me nigga!" Angel screeched pinching his hand.

"Nah, you out here acting a fool, drunk and shit." Daniel snapped.

Angel tried to pull away, but he choked her harder. Then, she kneed him in the crotch. He let her go and she scurried away, hailing a cab. Daniel was hot on her hills, sliding into the backseat behind her. Angel folded her arms across her chest and stared out the window. He was still cradling his dick.

"Yo, you wilding and shit." He winced. "But wait til I get you back to this fucking room." He threatened through clenched teeth.

They walked through the lobby of the hotel, growling at each other and whispering obscenities. People were looking at them like they were Ike and Tina. When they stepped into the elevator, Daniel grabbed her by the arm and bit her on the ear.

"Let go!" she hit him on the arm.

He pushed her out of the opening doors and slammed her against the wall. "Shut up," he yelled, smacking her across the face.

Angel stood there with her mouth open as he pulled her by the hair and down the hall to their room. The door opened, and he shoved her onto the bed. She tried to roll out of his reach, but he grabbed her by the leg.

"Fuck you think you going? Don't you ever put your fucking hands on me!" he slapped her.

Angel had never been so scared in her life. She reached up to hit him but her held her arms down and continued to smack her. When he was tired he stepped off and went into the bathroom. Angel balled up on the bed and caught her breath. A million thoughts were running through her head as the liquor was starting to ware off. She was trying to remember when he started treating her like this. Fuck, she thought as tears rolled down her cheeks. She listened as the shower water ran in the bathroom. She scooted to the edge of the bed and got her phone out of her purse to text Carla. She didn't know what else to do while the tears continued to fall from her eyes. She was bleeding and her hair was a mess.

When Daniel came out of the bathroom, she tucked the phone under the pillow and slid off the bed.

Angel stared at her battered face in the mirror. She wasn't the girl he met she was turning into someone else, an insecure girl who would settle for this. He loves me, she started to wipe her lip. He's drunk. She closed her eyes, remembering all the nights her mother would be soaking in the tub after her father had beat her. She cried, knowing that there were only a few ways out of this. She looked over her shoulder at the door when she heard him moving around in the room. She turned on the shower and cleaned herself up. Don't do that shit again, you going to lose a good man, she heard her mother's voice in her head. She wrapped herself in a towel and met Daniel back in the room. He was posted up in the bed cradling a bottle of Hennessey and a cigarillo. She climbed into the covers and reached for the remote.

"Yo," he said, blowing a cloud of smoke. "I love you."

She smiled and replied, "I know."

Angel tried to sleep but she just laid there with her eyes closed. Her face hurt on one side and she was still trying to figure out why she was still lying in the bed with him. He snuggled up to her and wrapped his arms around her waist. She cringed at his touch. She wanted to crawl out of the bed and leave him there, but she knew that it would probably make him angry. Where did she have to go anyway. So, she stayed as still as possible and prayed that the trip would go by quickly.

The next morning, Daniel wasn't there when she woke up. She looked around the room and got out of the bed to check in the bathroom. He wasn't there, either. Then, a knock came to the door. She frowned and tiptoed to look out the peephole. It was room service. She opened the door.

"I didn't order anything."

The waiter looked at the receipt. "Daniel Jones?"

"That's my boyfriend."

"Yes, he ordered this." She said and smiled.

Angel let her push the cart into the room. It was a tray of fruit, bacon, eggs, pancakes and chocolates. Angel closed the door and picked up the card. Daniel said he was sorry and that he wanted to make her feel like the princess she was. Another knock came to the door. It was a lady carry a suit back and a bunch of other stuff.

"Angel?" she smiled.

"Yes? What's all this?"

"You're scheduled for a make-over."

"Make-over?" Angel laughed coyly.

They entered the room with a dozen pairs of shoes, dresses, and a stylist. Daniel was really trying to make up for how he had treated her the night before. Angel had butterflies in her stomach as she read another card from him. He wanted her to meet him at a restaurant downtown. She picked the prettiest dress of the lot and headed downstairs to the lobby of the hotel where a driver a waited her. She was feeling like Vivian Ward in Pretty Woman. Damn, she shook her head and smiled as she slid into the backseat.

The town car pulled up to a restaurant called Chi Bella. The driver pulled her out of the back seat and she walked up to the door where someone showed her to their table.

He was sitting there in a three-piece suit, looking like a piece of meat. It worked, she damn near forgot about the ass whipping he laid on her the night before. They enjoyed a candle lit dinner with wine and laughter.

Then they took a walk on the Riviera. She leaned over, looking at the waves and he squeezed her from behind. She smiled as his lips brushed against her neck.

"I love you…" Daniel whispered in her ear.

"I love you, too. I'm sorry." She offered, turning to face him.

Daniel swallowed hard and stepped back. "I was tripping," he admitted.

Angel closed her eyes and said, "I know what I saw. I'm not blind Daniel."

"You know what you think you saw, but that ain't what you saw." He tried to explain.

Angel shook her head. "What? That doesn't even make sense."

"Angel," he touched her on the arm. "I'm sorry, okay? And it won't happen again. Everything got out of hand."

"Damn right." Angel touched the side of his face. "I just don't…"

"I'm sorry." He kissed her on the lips.

The ride back to the hotel was complete with tongue action, hugs and touching. Daniel was feeling her up all the way to the room. He laid her on the bed and pushed her dress up to her hips and pulled her panties to the side. She arched her back, his tongue dipping in and out of her warmth. She put her hand on the back of his head and wrapped her legs around his neck. She was moaning and groaning, wiggling her body.

"Oh, baby." She cried, cumming in his mouth. "Please." She whined.

"Don't cry now," he warned, biting down on her pussy. "This my pussy?" he asked.

"Yes, it's yours baby."

"Cum for me then," he whispered, fingering her while sucking on her clit.

Her legs were shaking, and she was crying as her love overflowed. He stood up and slid is penis into her wetness. He was pounding on her, squeezing her titties and sucking on her neck. She wrapped her legs around his waist and took all the dick he was giving her. Then, they laid there and their wetness, panting from the passion they had shared. She ran her hand over his waves, feeling that she had fallen in love with a man who reminded her of her daddy.

Chapter Eight

The next morning, Angel was awake before him. She ordered breakfast and turned on the television. There was a marathon of Law and Order SUV on. She was smacking on a piece of toast when Daniel stirred in his sleep. He put his arm on her thigh and reached up to kiss her.

"Good morning, beautiful." He smiled at her.

Her face was healing nicely, and he was reminded of the monster he had turned into. He was sorry, but he knew that if she ever got out of line with him again, he would whip that ass again. He was a man and he would not tolerate disrespect from any woman. Angel was beautiful, even with the scars from the accident and he didn't want to ruin her face, but she had to understand that he was a man.

He rolled over in the bed and picked up the half smoked blunt form the ashtray. He lit it and took a pull as he stood up.

"You want some?" she pointed to the tray of food.

"That's aight you enjoy your breakfast and I'm gone go take a shower," he headed in the bathroom turned on the water.

Angel remember the dick he had given her the night before. She wanted some more of that good thing. She took a bite of her bacon and a quick sip of orange juice and headed to the bathroom. She undressed and got in with him. He put his arms around her and she started kissing his chest. He grabbed her butt with both hands pulling her closer than leaned down and put her tittie in his mouth and began to play with her pussy. He pressed her body against the wall and got down on his knees water running down his back. He kissed on her stomach and lift her leg up and begin licking her clit. She reached down and grabbed his head holding on tight and then closed her eyes and breathed heavily. As she began to cum she squeezed his head he then came up kissed her. Still dripping they went at it again blaze up in the air and then was giving her the he came shortly afterwards

"Damn you gone have a nigga chilling in the room all weekend." Daniel hissed.

She took her finger and slid it across his chest.

"That's not so bad is it?"

"Naw it ain't, but I want to go out and hit the streets." He told her.

"We can. It's not really much to do during the day, but I'm sure we can think of something." She got up and walked over to Daniel, pulled his drawls down and started stroking his dick. She caressed his balls before putting them in her mouth. She licked up and down before putting the tip in her mouth. She tried to see how much she could put in before she gagged. She slowly started going to work. Slob running down her mouth onto his dick, he put his hand on top of her head and started pushing it up and down. They went at it again then took a rest.

After a quick shower they both got dressed. Angel was dipped in a black jumper and he was fresh in a pair of Trues and tall cans. He smiled at her while she fixed her makeup in the mirror.

"Damn, girl, you fine." He smacked her on the butt.

Angel grinned and said, "I know, right?"

They went to the hotel bar, first. Daniel ordered four shots of Henny and she helped him guzzle them down. Then, they went to a local club. Of course, there was a bunch of bad bitches and a couple of sexy ass bearded niggas. Angel was feeling sexy, but she wasn't trying to have a repeat of the night before. She stayed mellow, dancing to a couple of songs and keeping her eyes on Daniel. Vegas was a city that never slept so Daniel and Angel partied until the wee hours of the morning. By the time they headed back to the hotel her head was spinning and she was stumbling all over the place. Daniel held her by the waist and guided her through the halls. She laughed and giggled as she fell on the bed.

"I got a headache so bad." She grunted, pushing her shoes off.

"Just lay down, I got you." Daniel told her.

"I think I drunk too much," Angel sighed as she puts her hand on her face.

"I told you slow down them drinks would catch up to you." Daniel pulled the straps off her shoulders and pulled her clothes off.

"I know I'm sorry. Just let me lay down for a minute and I'll come back out with you." Angel whispered, closing her eyes.

Daniel shook his head and said, "Okay take your time lay down. I ain't going nowhere."

Before she fully drifted to sleep Daniel had snuck out the door. A couple hours have passed, and Daniel was still gone. Angel opened her eyes still kind of blurry looking around the room. Just then the door opened, and Daniel walked in, but before she could call out to him it was a tap at the door. Angel laid there trying to listen.

"What are you doing here?" he whispered.

"Here you left this. Call me sometimes," A girl said.

Angel tried not to react and pretend she was still asleep.

"You know I will." He nodded as he shut the door.

By the time he turned around Angel was sitting up on the bed. She was staring directly at him with fire in her eyes. She knew damn well he wasn't bringing hoes to the room door. She wanted to pounce on his ass, but she knew that he was quick with the hands. She folded her arms across her chest.

"Who was that?" She snapped

"Who was what?" Daniel put his watch on the dresser and glared at her.

"Don't play stupid Daniel." Angel's legs swung over the side of the bed. "Who was at the door?"

"Oh, that was the housekeeper." Daniel sat on the edge of the bed and started to take his shoes off.

"This time of night? What did she want?" Angel slid next to him on the bed.

"I dropped my watch and she brought it back up to me." He took off his shirt. "That's all look at my baby being paranoid you got me I ain't going nowhere." He reached for a kiss.

But Angel backed up. "Mm hmm you think I'm stupid?"

"Naw baby I think you beautiful." He caressed her leg.

Angel rolled her eyes and he looked at her funny. "You don't believe me?"

"I guess." She shook her head and pulled the covers back. Her head was still spinning so she was not about to get into it with him.

Daniel snapped his teeth and went into the bathroom. Angel pulled the covers over her head and closed her eyes.

"Yeah he up to something." She mumbled.

The next morning Angel went off to do her own thing. She wanted to enjoy her last day without any interruptions. She went to a show, did a little shopping and enjoyed a nice lunch by herself. After she was done she headed back to the room to spend some alone time with Daniel. She got to the floor and as she approached the room door she heard voices coming from inside. She squinted and pressed her ear against the door.

"Damn," Daniel hissed. "That neck."

"You like it, poppy?" A chick asked and then made loud slurping noises.

Angel's bottom lip curled up. She pulled out her key card and still listened as Daniel moaned and the Spanish girl said something. Angel shoved the key into the door and it made a beeping sound.

"What the fuck?" Daniel jumped up and pushed the girl out of his lap.

She looked like a deer caught in headlights. She grabbed the sheet and wrapped it around her frail body. Tears weld up in Angel's eyes.

"What you doing?" she asked him, as the tears fell. "Can't leave you alone for one…"

"Angel…" Daniel started. "I was just…"

"In here letting this bitch suck your dick!" Angel yelled as the girl scurried out of the room.

"Angel, chill. I needed…"

"I fuck you and suck you. What you needed that bitch for? Huh? You just wanna see me mad huh? First your bitch ass fucked up my face and now you in here with this hoe?" Angel tossed her phone at him.

"Fuck!" Daniel jumped up and grabbed her by the wrist. "I told you it ain't nothing."

"Where the condoms at? You was fucking this bitch raw?" Angel asked.

Daniel snapped his teeth and pushed her against the wall. "Chill the fuck out."

Angel mushed him in the face. He wrapped his hands around her neck and choked her.

"Let me go!" She screamed. "I'm tired of this shit. I wanna go home!" Angel cried.

He let her go and she slid down the wall, crying. She sat there for a few minutes and continued to say that she wanted to go home. Daniel was walking around the room, snatching up all her shit. Their trip wasn't over for a few days but if she wanted to go home she was more than welcome to. He shoved her stuff into a suitcase.

"Get the fuck on then! Stupid ass bitch!" he yelled. "You make me fucking sick with all this crying and shit."

Angel looked up at him with hate in her eyes. She slowly stood up and gathered her stuff.

"Fuck your nigga." She took her suit case and rolled it out of the room. She was just about to the elevator door when Daniel stepped out of the room, wrapped in a towel.

His muscles were budging out and he was looking like the nigga she met in the restaurant.

"Baby it's not what you think." He said from the door. "This all a misunderstanding."

Angel looked up at him with disgust. "How can you stand there and say that? Of course, it's what I think. You were getting your dick sucked what else was it? And you going to put me out?"

"Look you want me to tell you the truth?" he asked. "

"Naw I want you to lie to me." She stood there with her hands on her hips. Of course, I want you to tell me the truth." She stepped toward him.

"Alright, come back in here and I'ma tell you." He grabbed her bags. "When you dozed off last night I went back to the club for a few drinks. She was still there and offered me another lap dance."

"So, the first time wasn't good enough?" Angel rolled her eyes and plopped down on the bed.

He hunched his shoulders, sitting down next to her. He was like all the other niggas she dated. He wanted to have his cake and eat it too. He wanted to be able to do whatever he wanted without consequence. She sat there, thinking that she should haul ass out of there, but something was holding her back.

"I mean what the fuck? You bring me all the way out here to embarrass me?" Angel cried.

Daniel kissed his teeth, "Embarrass you?"

"Yes." She leaned back on the bed and sighed. "How you turn into this? It's like Dr. Jekyll and Mr. Hyde." She shook her head. "One minute you cool and the next you flying off the handle. I never thought I have to be scared of you, Daniel."

"Scared of me?" He touched her on the side of the face and she flinched. "I'm sorry baby. I don't know why I get so angry, but I love you til death."

"I love you, too but at what cost?" Angel looked him in the eyes. "You keep embarrassing me."

"How I embarrass you Angel? You tripping." Daniel snatched away. "Maybe you should go on home." He stood up.

"Seriously?" Angel hopped to her feet. "You ain't shit."

"Yeah seriously cause this shit is irritating." Daniel snapped. "Go on." He pointed to the door.

He ain't bout to kick me out of this mother fucker another time. She grabbed her shit and bounced, not looking back. Within a few hours she had booked a flight and was back home. Angel didn't know who the fuck Daniel thought she was, but that dick wasn't that good. She was glad to be home and in her own bed. She opened the cooler and pulled out a bottle of wine to go through the eighty messages he had left.

Chapter Nine

The next day, Carla and Trina came over to hear all about her trip. She wanted to vent to her friends, but she knew they would never understand. They were there for all the shit she had been through and at heart they wanted what was best for her, but Angel was going to do what she wanted to do anyway. She sat on the couch with a glass of wine.

"Tell us all about your lil freak nick," Carla grinned as she tapped the seat next to her for Angel to sit down.

"It was straight." Angel didn't really want to get into the truth.

"Straight?" Trina laughed. "Bitch you just came back from Vegas and that's all it was?"

"I mean for the most part everything was good." Angel lied, praying they didn't notice all of the makeup she was wearing. "It's just that," she paused. "Naw it's nothing we had a blast girl it was so much fun." Angel laughed.

"Well what was all that then?" Carla smirked. "The shit you was texting me?" she pulled out her phone.

"Dang Carla the girl said it was nothing. Now tell us all about it." She leaned in.

"Ok we went to a couple shows, played at the casinos and hit a few clubs."

"Ooh did y'all go to the tittie bars? I heard those the shit in Vegas."

"Yeah we did," she mumbled under her breath.

"Well how was it?" Carla sat there with her mouth opened. She wanted to hear all about the trip but something about Angel's demeanor was telling her that there was something she wasn't telling them.

"She was pretty," Angel shrugged, "with her lil ugly titties."

"Wait. What? Who was pretty Angel?" Trina laughed sat

up in her seat.

"Ugh if I tell y'all anything more y'all will just jump to the wrong conclusion."

"I mean hell what conclusion can we jump to Angel?"

She took a deep breath. She was on the verge of crying because if she told them all of what Daniel did to her while she was in Vegas, they would flip the script. Her momma always told her that you can't tell your friends all your business. She leaned back in her seat and took another sip of her drink.

"It wasn't nothing we went to a tittie bar. He had a lap dance and he started feeling on the girl titties."

"Wait a minute" Trina's bottom lip curled into a frown as she started throwing her hands around. "This mutha'fucka had the audacity to take you to some bar and be feeling all up on some bitch in front of you?"

"See this is why I didn't want to tell y'all, because of this right here." Angel threw her hands up.

"Angel we're you're friends. We're not judging you or anything we're just worried about you."

"Well you don't have to," she placed her drink on the table. "I'm fine. I got everything under control."

Trina sat back in her seat and crossed her legs. She was salty because a part of her knew that Angel wasn't telling them everything. She looked over at Carla, who looked like she was thinking the same thing, and then fixed her eyes on Angel.

"Ok Miss I got everything under control. What happened next?" Carla questioned.

"Nothing. He reassured me that it was nothing," Angel told them.

Trina and Carla both smacked their lips. Angel was lying through her teeth. Carla thought about the messages she had sent her and knew that Daniel had probably smacked her around.

"Then we made up." Angel grinned, "I mean what

reason do I have not to trust him?"

Carla rolled her eyes, "Well I hope you know what you're doing Angel."

"I do Carla, and you have nothing to worry about."

"Okay cause you know I'm always here for you." She got up to hug her.

Angel sighed. "I know." She laughed.

These were her girls. Although they didn't always get along, she knew they wouldn't stare her wrong.

"And you know I'm always here for you too, and ready to beat somebodies ass." They all burst into laughter.

"Trina, you stay ready to pop off." Carla shot her eyes at her.

"You know it, but I'm gone catch y'all later" Trina said as she grabbed her purse.

Angel squinted her eyes, "Where you off to?"

"Oh," Trina pulled out her keys. "I'm going to get my nails done then out to eat with this guy name Lamont."

"You know you keep a tribe," Carla says sarcastically.

"Shit I got to." Trina laughed, her hand on the doorknob, "They got to pay to lay up with Trina. I'll see y'all later."

"Bye." Carla and Angel waved.

"Now that she's gone, how are you really doing?"

"I told you I was fine." Angel tried to convince Carla. "It was just a little misunderstanding that's all."

"Misunderstanding? Yeah on his part. I knew he was going to be trouble ever since you met him. I mean who grabs someone's hand to talk to them? That's not how a real man will get your attention, but you love them hood niggas. You and Trina." Carla sat down on the couch.

"See there you go," Angel shook her head.

"All I know is you sent me some disturbing text and that your eye is swollen under that makeup." Carla called her out.

Angel touched her eye and put her head down. Tears finally started to fall. "I couldn't believe it." She whimpered. "He hit me because he was fucking with some bimbo." She shook her head.

"Oh, baby." Carla scooted close to her on the couch and wrapped her hands around her shoulders.

Angel was crying because she had been a fool once again. She was pissed at herself. How could I let him do this to me? I deserve better, don't I? she sobbed hard, pressing her head into Carla's chest. Disappointment settled into her heart and the tears continued to flow as they sipped wine. Carla didn't judge her or place blame on her, she was only there to listen and support her.

Carla learned a long time ago not to get in the middle of domestic disputes. Some will take your help and others would turn on you. She could recall a time Angel got involved with this little drug dealer from their old neighborhood. He had held her up in the bedroom and damn near stomped the life out her. Carla, being the good friend that she was, busted into the room and hit him in the head with a pan but Angel was upset with her in the days that followed, and they didn't speak for months. She loves her friend, but she won't be getting in the middle. All she could really do is pray for her and give some advice.

"Girl," Angel patted her on the leg, "you know that nigga kicked me out? And told me to go home alone?"

Carla's mouth dropped, and she rolled her eye, "Now, you know better, and you know you can do better."

"Chile. I hurried my ass on home and ain't answered his messages since."

Carla snapped her teeth, "Tuh, like that's supposed to be some victory."

"Girl," Angel stood up, "he ain't finna kick me out and then come lay up."

"You crazy as hell," Carla slipped.

Angel darted her eyes at her and put her hands on her

hips. "Girl, you can go."

"Oh, so you putting me out?" Carla was surprised.

"Yup. Don't let the door knob hit you where the good lord split you."

Angel didn't have to tell Carla twice. She snatched up her purse and quickly left the apartment. Carla was pissed off, but Angel always showed her true colors when it came to a man. Carla couldn't be mad at anyone but herself because she still considered her a friend. She climbed into her car and sped off. Stupid bitch, she thought, turning up Bodak Yellow on the radio.

Angel plopped down on the couch, folding her legs under her butt, and turned on the TV. Her phone buzzed on the table as she flipped through the channels. It was yet another message from Daniel. His flight had just landed, and he wanted to apologize for all the shit he did to her in Vegas. Angel grinned, knowing that the makeup was about to be popping. He would buy her a necklace or something and take her to some fancy restaurant. She was waiting for him to tell her to come through.

"Oh, so what you bout to get into?" she asked.

"Shit chilling with the fellas, what you doing?"

"Wishing I could see you."

"Oh well that wish can easily be granted," Daniel texted back. "I'll come by there when I leave here."

"Okay baby see you, then." She hung up the phone then watched a little TV.

She had dozed off and missed a couple calls from Daniel. Then she was startled by the knocking at the door. She looked through the peephole and opened the door.

"You ain't see me calling you all them times?" He shouted as she stepped back.

"I was in here sleep," Angel cover her mouth as she yawned and reached for her phone "Boy, you only called me twice."

"Well it was one too many unanswered," Daniel went into the kitchen for a beer.

Angel was walking around him, straightening up. He licked his lips, leaning against the counter.

"Damn, you fine as hell." He told her.

"Oh, really?" Angel bent over to pick something up from the floor. "You like how my ass shaped?"

"Hell yeah." He pulled her into his arms and leaned in to kiss her.

Angel sucked on his bottom lip and wrapped her arms around his neck. He picked her up and carried her to her bedroom. Laying her on the bed, Daniel slowly kissed her all over her body but when he got down between her legs, he suddenly stopped. Angel laid there, waiting for something to happen, but when it didn't she sat up in the bed.

"Daniel?" she looked down and he was slumped over the edge of the bed. "What the fuck? Daniel?" she tried to turn him over, but he was too heavy. "Oh my god!" Angel panicked, picking up the phone to dial 911. "My boyfriend... he...oh my god! Send someone." She watched in horror as he started to shake uncontrollably. "I think he's having a seizure."

About ten minutes later, the paramedics arrived to take Daniel to the hospital. Angel sat in the back of the truck, holding his hand. They were asking her about his history and if he had taken anything. She was completely clueless. She didn't know anything except his last name. she had never seen him have a seizure before and that shit scared the hell out of her. As the ambulance rushed to the hospital he went into convulsions again.

"Baby," she cried, praying that he would be okay.

It seemed like hours had passed before a doctor came into the room. They administered some medication and Daniel seemed to relax. Slowly, he opened his eyes and looked around the room.

"Daniel?"

"Angel? What happened?" he asked. "Where are we?"

"In the hospital. Boy, you scared the fuck out of me." She tapped him on the shoulder. "Why didn't you tell me you have Epilepsy?"

"I…. I…." then, the convulsions started again.

A bunch of nurses ran into the room and pushed Angel out. She was horrified, standing outside of the room as they worked on him. They told her to wait in the waiting area. With shaky hands she called Carla.

At first Carla wasn't going to answer the phone. She figured Angel had let Daniel come over and he had beat her ass again. She rolled over in the bed and ignored the first few calls. Angel wasn't letting up and the buzzing noise was annoying, so Carla sat up and pressed talk on the phone.

"Hello?"

"Carla? Please don't hang up. I'm sorry about earlier." Angel said. "I'm at the hospital. Daniel had a seizure and…" she cried.

"Girl, you calling my phone about that nigga?" Carla rolled her eyes.

"I need you. I need my friend. I'm here alone and I'm scared."

"You shoulda thought about your friend before you kicked me out of your apartment."

"I'm sorry, okay?" Angel whimpered. "Please, come sit with me."

"Girl, bye." Carla hung up.

The phone buzzed with a text from Angel telling her what hospital she was in. Carla looked over at her man and thought about laying back down.

"Damn," she whispered into the darkness, pulling the blanket back. "She better be lucky I'm saved." Carla climbed out of bed and throw on some clothes.

Angel was pacing back and forth in the waiting room

when Carla arrived. Carla sat down and folded her legs. She was only there for support because she was still pissed with Angel. If it was one thing she didn't like it was a woman who treated her friends like shit when her man was dead wrong. She folded her arms across her chest and waited for Angel to sit down.

"So, what are the doctors saying?"

"He has Epilepsy. They say he hasn't been taking his meds." She shook her head. "I didn't see him taking no meds."

"Girl," Carla shook her head.

"He was down there bout to go to work and then it just stopped."

Carla burst into laughter. "Y'all was fucking and this nigga had a seizure?"

"Yes," Angel tapped her leg, "lower your voice." She looked around.

"That's some wild shit!" Carla laughed some more. "How he die?"

"On top of me," Angel finished the famous line from, The Color Purple. "You a whole fool."

"Nah, y'all shouldn't have been being nasty." Carla couldn't contain her laughter. "That's wild." She shook her head.

Angel was a little embarrassed. The doctor finally came out to talk to her. He stated that Daniel was going to be okay but that he should always take his medications when he is supposed to, even if he feels fine. They ordered a few tests and admitted him to the hospital until the results came back. After three hours, he was assigned to a room and resting comfortably. Angel sat by his side while Carla went home to get ready for work.

When he opened his eyes, he reached out for her hand. "I'm sorry to put you through this."

"Oh baby." Angel whispered, "I'm just glad you're okay."

"Damn, I don't remember nothing." He closed his eyes.

"We were getting ready to do the nasty and then, you just started shaking all over my damn floor."

Daniel looked at her strangely and then, the two shared a laugh. "Yo, that's a wild ass story."

"You sound like Carla. I don't find it funny at all." Angel shook her head. "I thought your ass was dying."

"Nah, I ain't ready to check out just yet. I mean, I did see the light and my Momma was at the end of the tunnel. She smiled and waved but…"

Angel leaned back in her chair with her head down. "I didn't know we had that in common."

"Your mother died, too?"

"Yeah, when I was nineteen." Angel recalled.

"My mom was in an accident. A car accident so they say but the autopsy revealed she was shot in the head."

Angel sat up and stared at him. "My mother was shot in the head too, only difference is I was standing there while my father held the gun to her head. She was crying, begging him to stop but he shot her right in front of me and then shot and killed himself." Angel cried.

Daniel reached for her hand again, but she pulled away. All the memories that she had suppressed came flooding back. She jumped up from the chair and ran from the room. She was a damaged girl and perhaps, that's why she accepted such foolishness from him. She accepted Daniel's lies and mistreatment because that was all she knew.

Angel got into her car and drove home. A part of her wanted to be there for him but she needed sometime. Will he ever change? Will he ever make her feel like the queen she knew she was? A man doesn't love a woman unless he hurts her, Angel thought about all the times her mother had said that. Men are much different than women—hotheaded. With tears streaming down her cheeks, Angel pulled into her parking space and got out of the car.

"I will not let that be me." She said, putting the key into the door.

Chapter Ten

After a week Daniel was released from the hospital. He claimed that he didn't want to be home alone, so he's been bunking in Angel's bed since. Like a good girlfriend, she's been waiting on him hand and foot. She'd cook and bring him breakfast, lunch and dinner. Then, she would run his shower and walk him to it. Apparently, Daniel liked all of the attention. He was taking his meds and treating her like he had when they first got together. Her saving his life seemed to have changed him.

As she helped him into the shower, he smiled up at her and said, "Thank you, Beautiful. Why don't you shower with me?" he asked.

"Oh," Angel eased from under his arm, "I'm only nursing you back to health."

"What? So, you ain't my baby no more?" Daniel frowned.

"Uh," she leaned back on the sink, "I thought we talked about this. The doctor said you will be back to yourself within two weeks and by then you will have to get out of my house," she said as a matter of fact.

"You tripping." Daniel snapped his teeth. "There are plenty of bitches out there that would kill for a nigga like me. You out here eating good, looking good but you ungrateful as fuck."

"Ungrateful? You want me to stand here and let you kill me? Nah, nigga you got me fucked up!" Angel shouted. "You can get your shit and get out now!"

"I ain't going no mu'fucking where. Now, raise on up outta here so I can wash my dick!"

Angel rolled her eyes and left the bathroom. Daniel didn't understand that she meant what she said, she needed a break from their relationship, but she would take care of him while he was sick. He was getting on her nerves now, though. He was trying to do too much. She wasn't ready to let him back into her heart and she still hadn't forgiven him for what happened in Vegas.

Daniel came from the bathroom and sat across from her on the bed. He lifted a blunt to his lips and lit it as he leaned back on the bed. "Where the fucking remote?"

"I don't know." Angel shrugged her shoulders.

"Well find the shit. Do something useful."

Angel snapped her teeth and folded her arms across her chest. "Guess we ain't going to be watching shit cuz I ain't looking for no remote."

"You been talking to them bitches too much thinking you could talk to me like that!" Daniel raised his hand and smacked her across the face.

Angel sat there, stunned. "Oh, hell no!" she screeched, attacking him.

Daniel flung her on the bed, putting all of his body weight on her as he held his hands around her neck.

"Get the fuck off me!" She swung at his head until he let her go.

She scurried from his reach and ran out of the room. She grabbed her purse and went to get in her car. She needed to get as far away from him as possible before one of them ended up dead. She called Carla.

"Where you at girl?" she asked.

"Home. You know it's my day off."

"I'm coming by." Angel told her.

"Bring me a soda. I'm thirsty as hell."

"Girl you in the way. Aight, I'll see you in a minute."

After going to the store, Angel arrived at Carla's apartment, using her key to get in. Carla was curled up on the couch, watching a Lifetime Movie. She looked up at Angel and shook her head. She was ready to say some slick shit but clearly her friend was not in the mood. Angel sat the soda on the table and took a seat on the couch.

"I am sick of that nigga." Angel huffed.

"I told you," Carla cut her eyes at her. "I told you not to let that nigga come there."

"I know but I was trying to treat him how I would want someone to treat me."

"Man listen…"

"Girl, he in my house cussing me out, hitting me…"

"Hitting you?"

"Yes," Angel whispered.

"You want me to get Twan to go over there? You know he don't mind blasting a nigga."

Angel shook her head. The last thing she needed was to get put out of her apartment over some bullshit. She wanted to handle Daniel on her own, but it was getting to be too much. Carla rubbed her leg and then took a sip of her soda.

"Girl, I just would hate to see you get really hurt."

"I know, Girl." Angel touched her hand. "For now, I'ma just sit here with you and watch sappy ass movies."

Chapter Eleven

Finally, Daniel was out of her house and Angel was free to do whatever she wanted. It was Friday night and she was heading out for a night on the town with her girls, Carla and Trina. She was dressed in a cute pair of daisy dukes and a baby doll tee. Her hair was pulled into a bun and she had already drank two glasses of Long Island Ice Tea. She heard Carla beep the horn and grabbed her purse and keys from the counter.

Surprisingly, when she opened the door, Daniel was standing there. She looked him up and down and tried to brush pass him.

"Where you think you going?" he asked, grabbing her arm.

Angel put her hand on his and pushed him, "Get off me."

"Yo," he put his lips near her neck, "you always going to belong to me."

Angel's phone rang in her hand, it was Carla. "Girl, what's taking you so long?"

"I'm coming." Angel answered, staring at Daniel.

"Hurry up. Ladies in free before 10 and it's already 9:15." Carla hung up.

Angel glared at Daniel. "I ain't your girl no more." She walked passed him.

When she got in the car Carla turned up the music and sped off. They were rapping along to a Cardi B song and feeling amped up for the evening. Suddenly, Angel was quiet as she stared out the window. She turned in her seat and looked out the rear window to get a better look. "Bitch, what's wrong?" Carla frowned.

"That nigga following us." She said.

Carla looked through the rear-view window, confused; she didn't see anyone. "Girl you being paranoid."

She pulled into the parking lot adjacent to the club.

Angel looked over her make-up in the mirror and then, got her ID out of her purse. They walked up to the line where Trina was already waiting. She snapped her fingers and danced to whatever beat was coming from the club. They reached the front of the line as Angel looked around for Daniel. She knew that she saw him following them. Even though she felt eerie, she shook it off and went into the crowded club. It was jammed pack and the music was jumping. Angel was already a little wavy from the Long Island Ice Teas she had already drank but she ordered two more at the bar. Quickly, she tossed them back because she was trying to shake the feeling she had. Her eyes scanned the crowd, but she didn't see Daniel. Carla and Trina were on the dance floor, shaking their asses to an old school club banger.

"This my shit!" Carla huffed as she approached the bar. She waved down the bartender. "Lemme get a rum and coke."

"You old as hell drinking that dry shit!" Angel teased.

"Oh, shut the hell up!" Carla laughed.

Trina ordered a straight mango Ciroc. She sat down next to Angel and slowly sipped. She thought she saw Daniel in the crowd, but she wasn't sure, so she didn't say anything to Angel. She looked at her friend and then back at the crowd.

"You okay?" Carla asked. "Trina? Are you okay?"

Trina snapped back, taking another sip. "I'm cool. Y'all ready to have some fun or what? I ain't bout to be sitting down all night." Trina slid off the stool. "I came out to show my ass."

"I know that's right." Angel grabbed her by the hand and pulled her to the dance floor with Carla a few steps behind them.

It was like old times. It had been a while since they'd been out at the club together. Angel, Carla and Trina were having a blast, creating new memories. Carla was really starting to feel her drinks, so she pulled out her phone and texted her man. She told him that she was horny and really wanted to fuck. She was grinning hard when Angel caught her attention.

"Who you talking to?"

"My baby." Carla slid the phone back into her pocket.

"I thought this night was about us."

"Hell, I still got to make that dick appointed." Carla slurred.

Angel looked at her strangely because she never talked like that. Trina scanned the crowd, thinking that she saw Daniel again.

"Hey," She pulled Angel close to her. "Are you and that boy still seeing each other?"

"Who Daniel?"

"Yeah."

"Naw, it's over between us, why you ask that?" Angel frowned.

Trina swallowed hard and closed her eyes really quick. "Aw, nothing. Just wondering."

"Oh okay. Girl you had me scared. He showed up at my house earlier and I thought I saw him following us." Angel admitted.

"Oh shit!" Trina gasped. "So that probably was him."

"What?"

"I saw a dude earlier that looked like him."

"Damn shame. He don't get that it's over." Angel shook her head. "I ain't tryna be like my momma. I wanna live."

"Girl, I know that's right." Carla butted in. "I will be right back."

"Where you going?" Trina and Angel asked at the same time.

"I'm going right over there." She pointed toward the bathroom.

Carla stepped into the Ladies Room where her boyfriend Twan was waiting in a stall. He pulled her in and wrapped his arms around her.

"Miss you!" he shoved his tongue down her throat as he felt all over her body.

"I missed you too baby." She pulled his belt loose and stroked his hardened dick.

Twan spun her around and pushed her against the door, pulling her pants down and sliding his dick into her. She held on to the door while he fucked her from behind. Carla was moaning and groaning, taking the dick. When they were done, she and Twan walked out of the bathroom hand in hand.

Daniel spotted her and approached her asking, "Where's Angel?"

"What are you doing here? She doesn't want to see you." Carla told him.

"Bitch…" he started but Twan stepped in front of Carla.

"This ain't what you want, Bruh."

"Fuck you mean? All I asked that bitch was where is my girl."

"Bruh, no need for all that base in your voice. She said Angel ain't fucking with you now move on." Twan told him.

"Fuck you think you is?" Daniel punched Twan in the face.

All hell was about to break loose. Twan and Daniel tussled while Carla went to get her girls. She knew that Twan was about that life and someone might not make it out of there alive. She and the girls headed outside of the club as the bouncers and armed security went to break the fight up.

"All I wanted was a night out with my girls. This is some straight bullshit." Angel cried. "That nigga crazy."

They waited for Twan to exit the club while Carla went to get her car. He stumbled out a few minutes later, holding his side. Blood was pouring between his fingers. He coughed, falling on the ground.

"Oh my god!" Trina and Angel leaned down beside him. "What happened?"

"That bitch ass nigga stabbed me." He winched in pain.

"I'm so sorry." Angel cried.

Carla jumped from the car and helped them put Twan in the backseat. When they got into the car she sped off. "I need to get you to a hospital."

"Nah, nah! Roll to the crib." Twan struggled to say.

"Nah, I'ma take you to the hospital. It looks bad Twan."

"Trust me Carla, I got this."

She hurried to get to the house, pulled into her drive way and they drug him inside. Carla pulled him into the bathroom and went to get a first aid kit. Angel cut his shirt off and Trina used a bottle to rinse the blood away, but it kept gushing out.

"What the fuck!" Trina yelled. "Damn Carla hurry up with that first aid kit."

Carla came into the bathroom and opened the kit. There were only bandages in it and some little alcohol pads. "What the fuck we supposed to do with this."

"You got some more bottled water, peroxide? Oh, and get me that needle and thread you use to tighten up that tired ass weave!" Trina packed the wound with a piece of his t-shirt.

"You going to sew it right here?" Angel asked holding up her bloody hands.

"What choice I got?" Trina looked at her, "You going to help me too."

There was blood everywhere. Beads of sweat were all over Twan's face and his eyes were rolling in the back of his head.

"You sure you don't wanna go to the hospital?" Angel asked as Carla came back with the supplies.

"Give him some water, this shit is going to hurt like

fuck!" Trina warned. "Bruh you gotta put a towel in his mouth cuz he going to be screaming his head off."

"Oh my god!" Angel yelled as blood started squirting out of the wound.

"Calm down!" Trina told her. "Take a breath.

"Bitch you act like this some normal shit. Ain't nothing normal bout this." Carla shook her head, trying to comfort Twan.

Trina got the bleeding under control. She cleaned the hair sewing needle with the peroxide and then, threaded it. She took a deep breath and started to sew the wound. As expected Twan was screaming at the top of his lungs and the blood was still squirting. Carla dapped his forehead with a towel and gave him more water. After twenty minutes, Trina was done sewing the wound. It looked like a professional had done it. She cut a piece of towel and taped it over the wound. Then, they helped Twan to the bedroom.

"What the fuck we going to do about all this blood?" Carla asked and then, the door bell rung.

"Who the hell is that?" the three women looked at each other.

They were all covered in blood. Carla went into the bedroom and looked out the window. "Fuck, it's the police."

"You live in this uppity ass neighborhood. One of your nosey ass neighbors done called the cops. Hurry up, change your clothes and go answer the door."

The bell rang again, "Police open up! We got a call about a disturbance."

"One second, officer." Carla answered in her calmest voice as she opened the door.

"Ma'am?" One of the officers said. "Is everything alright?"

"Yes," she answered, stepping aside to let them in.

"Well we got a call about screaming."

"Yeah, my husband stumped his big toe on the edge of the bed. You know how men are," she chuckled.

"On the edge of the bed?" He looked at her suspiciously. "Where is your husband now?"

"He's upstairs resting. I'm sorry that your time has been wasted."

"Well ma'am, all seems to be well. So, we will leave you to the rest of your night. Try to keep it down."

"We will and thanks for coming out so promptly." Carla smiled.

"No problem." The officer smiled, and they left.

Carla took a deep breath and ran up the stairs.

"Bitch!!!" she exclaimed looking out the curtain. "I just knew we was about to go to jail."

"'Ayo," Twan said from the bed. "Tell that nigga when I catch him I'ma put a hot one in his head."

"Damn," Angel sat in one of the chairs near the window. "This turned out to be one crazy ass night."

"Hell, yeah and now y'all going to help me get this house cleaned up."

"Aight." Trina headed toward the bathroom.

They removed everything including the bars of soap and then scrubbed the bathroom with bleach and ammonia. Carla kept new bathroom décor in her linen closet so while she changed it, Trina and Angel got rid of the trash.

"All we was tryna do is hang out. I might have to get a restraining order on him."

"Might? Nah, bitch, I'ma take you to the prescient myself. He dangerous, Angel." Trina told her as they met Carla in the kitchen.

"Right. Y'all staying here tonight. I don't need his ass popping up on you Angel and why didn't you tell me he was at your apartment?"

"Because I know how you get and now look."

"Right. This shit crazy and you better believe it's not

over.

Chapter Twelve

The moonlight shined into the living room as Angel sat on the couch flicking through the channels. It had been a few days since the incident at the bar and she hadn't heard from Daniel at all. In fact, she didn't know if he had made it out of the bar or not. Some piece of her was a little worried about him but she knew that it was in her best interest to stay away from him.

She dug her spoon into the carton of ice cream and her phone buzzed on the table. Picking it up, she was expecting a message from Carla or Trina, but it was from Daniel. He was saying that he missed her and wanted to see her. She put the phone back down on the table. She was not going to entertain him at all.

"As a matter of fact," she picked up the phone and scrolled to his number. "put his ass on block."

That ought to fix his crazy ass. She leaned back on the couch and took another scoop of ice cream. The phone buzzed again. Angel frowned. What the fuck?

Bitch, I know you see my fucking messages. If you don't fuck answer me, I'ma come burn that mu'fuckas down. You hear me? Huh, bitch? You know ain't no one ever going to love you like I love you, Angel. Answer the fucking phone!

Angel tossed the phone on the other side of the couch. Daniel is over the top. I need to go get that restraining order, Angel thought. The phone buzzed a few more times but Angel refused to look. She thought about the last time she saw him, the night he choked her. There was no way she would ever forgive him. The more she thought about it, the more she was reminded of the fateful day her mother and father died. Her mother was overtaken with guilt about her brother's death and her father could never understand. He was an angry drunk and he thought she loved her dead son more than she loved him, so he took her life and his. Daniel reminded her of her father, except he didn't need to be drunk to be abrasive.

"Damn," Angel sucked her teeth and went into the kitchen, "I thought I had more Long Island up in here." She shook the nearly empty bottle. "Guess I'm bout to take my ass to the store. I need something to keep my mind off this nigga."

She picked up her phone off the couch and saw that she had a missed call from Carla. She called her back as she walked out of the house. "Hey, chile."

"Hey, hunny. Was just wondering how you were doing."

"I'm okay." Angel said, uneasily.

Carla knew that Angel was holding back. She sighed into the phone and said, "Twan still in a lot of pain. I keep trying to get him to go to the hospital."

"And Daniel keeps calling me." Angel admitted as she climbed into her car. "I don't want to talk to him."

"You better not talk to his ass." Carla snapped her teeth. "You know he crazy."

"Girl I know." Angel pulled up in front of the liquor store. "Anyway, what you got planned for the day?"

"Nothing, chilling with my baby since he can't do much."

"Oh okay. I'm at this store getting a drink."

"A drink? Girl it's only Wednesday."

"So?" Angel looked down at the phone and saw a message from a private number.

I see you.

"Girl, I got to go." Angel hung up, looking over her shoulder.

She hurried to the counter and paid for her drink without taking a bag or her change. She practically ran out of the store and got into her car, speeding off. She saw a blue car behind her and tried to get home as quickly as possible. The car was still behind her when she parked but sped off when she stepped out. She quickly let herself into the house and then into her apartment. She put the chain on the door and went into the kitchen.

"Man." She took a deep breath and searched the cabinets for her anxiety pills. She needed to calm down. "I can't believe he's following me around like a lost puppy." She leaned on the counter.

There was a knock at the door that startled her from her train of thought. Angel tip toed to the door and looked out the peephole.

"Ms. Margret?"

"Dear, a package came for you."

"A package?" Angel opened the door. "Thank you, Ms. Margret." She took the package and closed the door.

It only had her name on it and no return address. Angel shook the box and then, thought about it being from Daniel.

"Oh hell no." she opened the front door and took the package to the side dumpster.

She hadn't ordered anything and knew that it could be dangerous if it was from Daniel. She wasn't going to take any chances. She called Trina and asked her to come with her to the police station the next day.

Chapter Thirteen

"Can't believe it's come to this." Angel said as they walked into the police station. "I hate it."

"Girl you gotta look out for you." Trina assured her that she was doing the right thing. "I have your back."

They approached the front desk and Angel explained that she wanted to get a restraining order against her ex-boyfriend who has been stalking her. They sat down for a few minutes before a detective came out.

"Good Afternoon, I'm Detective Ruiz." He extended his hand. "I understand that you are here to obtain a restraining order."

"Yes, sir."

"Okay, follow me." They went into a small office.

Detective Ruiz explained what a restraining order would entitle her to. He told her that Daniel wouldn't be allowed within 700 feet of her. She was told that he would be served a notice of the restraining order within five business days. She left there as afraid as she had been when she went in. Five days was a long time and there was no telling what extreme Daniel might go to. She asked Trina to stay with her for a little while, until she felt comfortable in the house. She called the phone company and had her number changed. She was through with him for real this time. She still didn't know that was in that package and in her heart, she believed that Daniel was capable of hurting her.

"It's going to be okay." Trina told her over a glass of Long Island.

"I sure hope so." Angel sighed. "I'm so frustrated. I should have just listened to Carla in the first place."

Trina crossed her legs and agreed, "He is a total nut case."

"Chile," Angel shook her head. "I probably just see my daddy in him."

"There you go with the psychology shit. If you know that much, then you should apply it."

Angel hunched her shoulder. "You right. I got to do better."

"Right, girl. You will come up out of this." Trina told her.

Angel prayed that the restraining order would keep him away. She wanted to move on with her life and not have to look over her shoulder, worrying if he would pop up and kill her. She regretted the day they met. Everything happened so fast. She met him and thought she was in love. The signs weren't clear at first, but she should have known the day he made her change her number that he was not who she thought he was. She thought she was in love though. She thought it was that staying home from work kind of love, that love you down so good you don't want to move kind of love. Daniel was loving her so good she almost forgot about the scars on her face and arms. She almost forgot about witnessing her mother die, literally and figuratively. She was crying—tears of fear and anger dropping from her eyes like raindrops in a forest. She couldn't understand why this was happening to her.

Trina wrapped her arms around her and held her tight while she sobbed. The merry-go-round was slowly stopping, and Angel's mind was not spinning. She could see clearly and suddenly she felt free. She took a deep breath and broke free from their hug.

"I'm going to cut my hair off." She announced, standing up.

Trina looked at her with bewilderment. "What? Girl you tripping."

"Nope." Angel went into the kitchen and grabbed the scissors. "I'm going to cut it off."

They went into the bathroom and Trina watched her cut all her hair off. "Now your ass out here looking crazy. I need you to sit your ass down and let me fix it."

"Do your magic girl. I am ready to be fab!" Angel laughed in a way that Trina hadn't heard in a while.

Trina chopped and curled her hair into a cute style and the two decided to go out for a while. Angel needed some fresh air. So, she got dressed in a pair of shorts and a tee. As they got into a car she got an idea.

"Let's go get a tat."

"A tat?" Trina looked at her crazily. "You scared of needles ain't you?"

"Yea, but bitchhhhh let's do it. We ain't getting younger."

"Tight but don't start crying and shit when it hurt."

"Shut up. Ohhh Carla going to be mad as hell."

"She a hag anyway." Trina laughed.

Angel swatted her on the shoulder. "Don't talk about my friend."

"You got that right, your friend. I could only imagine her face when the cops were at the door."

Angel laughed, too. "She was probably fixing to piss in her pants."

"Damn right."

Trina parked the car and they went into the tattoo shot. Angel was starting to get nervous and have second thoughts but as she looked through the artist's book, she spotted something that would be perfect.

"Oh shit, bitch, I'ma bout to get my nipples pierced." Trina announced.

"What? Now bitch you tripping." Angel laughed.

"I'm dead serious." Trina chuckled. "I heard niggas love that shit."

"You crazy as hell. I'm just going to start with this." Angel pointed at a picture in the book.

Angel was scared of needles but decided that she would chuck it up and let her fear go. She had been fearful of a lot of things in life but now she was trying to conquer that fear.

She didn't want to be held back by it any longer. After paying the booking fee, they sat patiently waiting on their turns. Trina went first, getting both of her nipples pierced. Angel was shaking but relaxed a little when he started on the tattoo. When they were finished the pair went to Gerri's to grab a drink and some grub. It was a small dimly lit bar and grill in the downtown area.

"Girl, I appreciate this." Angel told Trina as she sipped her Long Island.

"Anytime. I'm glad to see you finally getting back to you."

Angel smiled and replied, "I know right. I don't plan on going back to misery anytime soon." She shook her head.

Angel was relieved, finally. She had a new outlook on life and she wanted to move forward. In a way, she was proud to have finally stood up for herself. She had been in an abusive relationship before and would probably still have been in it if he hadn't been arrested on unrelated charges. It was a vicious cycle of settling. Watching her mother suffer had taught her that suffering was a part of love. Now, Angel was clear; love shouldn't hurt. She wasn't searching anymore though. She was going to live her best life.

Chapter Fourteen

Angel sat at her desk, chewing on a Chico Stick. Eight months had passed since her last encounter with Daniel. She had gotten a promotion at work and she and the girls were planning a trip to Dominican Republic. She was happy to say the least. Skin glowing, smile popping and hair damn near down her back. She was starting to see herself again— a tremendous growth.

"Hey Angel." Emanuel smiled, passing her desk.

"Hey." She replied, continuing to type.

Emanuel doubled back and stopped right in front of her. He leaned forward on her desk smelling like something out of GQ Magazine. She inhaled and tried not to act too interested.

"Some of us are going out for a drink tonight, wanna come?"

"Nah, thanks for asking." Angel told him.

"Come on, why not?"

Angel sighed, "I don't drink."

"Oh okay. But don't say I didn't invite you." He smiled and walked away.

Things were changing. Angel hadn't had a drink in months and that was okay. She vowed to make herself better and that meant having clear judgment. She hoped to remain sober for the rest of her life and if she did decide to have a glass of wine it would be in the comfort of her home.

She leaned back in her chair and read over the notes she had written in her report. She was excited about the first presentation she'd be giving to her boss in a few days. Her new position called for a lot of hard work and talking but Angel was confident in her ability to sign new deals for her company.

Angel packed up and left the office for the evening. She

couldn't wait to get home and take her bra off. That was definitely the best part of the day. She parked in her usual spot and headed into the apartment.

"Damn, it's breezy in here." Angel said aloud as she sat her bag down. "I know damn well I closed the window before I left." She examined the living room and then, walked through the house.

The bedroom window was opened. "Strange." She frowned, closing it.

She looked around the room and noticed a teddy bear on her pillow. She sat on the bed and took the bear in her hands. As she stared at it, the house phone rang. She put the bear on the bed and answered the phone.

"Angel?" a familiar voice spoke. "Please don't hang up."

"How did you get my number?"

"I been missing you." He said. "That's why I brought you a gift."

"You were in my house?" she looked down at the phone. "Stay away from me, Daniel."

"But Angel, I changed. Please hear me out."

"For what?" she asked, tears falling from her eyes.

"I love you. You know I do. I wanna be with only you. I know I fucked up but…"

"No… No. I am not doing this." She hung up.

Angel went to get the scissors and sliced the bear up. She couldn't believe that Daniel was still stalking her. Apparently, the restraining order was meaningless. Tears were steadily falling down her cheeks. I was doing so good, she thought, looking up at the ceiling. Why?

"I don't need this in my life right now," she said aloud. "I really don't."

Angel was not going to let Daniel take over her life. She grabbed her purse and went to her car were there was a note. She tore it to pieces and hopped in the car. What the hell? She banged on the stirring wheel. I can't believe this shit. She pulled up to a pawn shop. The clerk greeted her with a smile.

"How may I help you?"

"I'd like to buy a gun."

"A gun?" he asked. "What's a pretty lady like you need with a gun?"

"I guess the fact that I'm a pretty lady has gotten me into some trouble."

"Oh, I see. Well we have these for sale." He showed her to a cabinet with different calibers of guns.

Angel picked a small hand gun and thanked the clerk. She needed some protection from Daniel because the police weren't doing enough. She got into her car and checked to make sure the safety was on the gun. She drove off, heading to the mall. She needed to get a dress for Carla's anniversary party. It was an all-white affair. Angel was ready to party a little and hopped that she could get through the party without a drink.

As she drove, she called Trina to keep her company along the ride. She felt like someone was following her, but she didn't want to get herself all upset.

"Hello." Angel said, when she answered.

"What's up? Everything good? You ain't call me when you got home last night." Trina said.

"Something weird happened last night." Angel took a deep breath. "When I got home my windows were opened and there was a teddy bear on my bed."

"What?" Trina gasped. "From who? Daniel? He was in your apartment?"

"Yes, Girl, he climbed in the window and then, he called me asking if he could see me." Angel admitted.

"What? Girl, what the fuck?" Trina was flabbergasted. "You going to have to get a home security system or something in that bitch." Trina shook her head.

Angel sighed, "Girl I had to buy a gun."

"A gun? Girl, I'm really scared for you. He is a different kind of crazy. He needs to be locked up."

Angel started to cry. "He is taking over my life again, Trina. I don't know what to do."

"Girl," Trina took a deep breath, "you better make sure you have that gun on you at all times. Take that motherfucker to work, the shower, everywhere. You hear me?" Trina asked. "Please, girl."

"I know but who really wanna live like this?" She asked as she pulled into the mall. "I'm at this mall, about to go find something for Carla's party."

"Hell, why you ain't tell me that? I need to get something too." Trina snapped her teeth.

Angel laughed. "Girl you got shit in your closet with tags. You don't need to be at no mall." She got her purse and got out of the car.

"You're probably right. Hit me up when you get home. Be safe out there, okay?"

"Yea, girl. Love you."

"Love you too." They hung up.

Chapter Fifteen

Carla's house was filled with people, guest and carters. There were waiters and waitress dressed in black walking around with trays of wine and finger food while a live band played, and the people mingled. There was also an open bar and though Angel was contemplating ordering a Long Island Ice Tea, she stayed away from the bar. She scanned the room and found Trina, arm in arm with Jesse.

He was medium built with a fade, dressed in a white linen suite. Like Daniel, he had a full beard and a pearly smile. Angel approached them and kissed Trina on the cheek. She was dressed in a white pants suit.

"You looking good, girl." Angel complimented, leaning toward her ear. "Surprised your still with him.

"Girl," Trina whispered, "I like running up checks." He said through a smile.

"I know that's right." Angel slapped her hand.

Trina took a sip of her glass of champagne and curled up her lip. "I need something stronger than this. Let's go," she pulled Angel's hand.

Angel stayed put, pulling her arm back. She bit her bottom lip. It was tempting but she had to stick to the vows she had made to herself. It had been months since she had drunk any alcohol and she planned to keep it that way.

"No," she shook her head, "you go. I'll catch up with you in a minute."

"What?" Trina frowned. "You don't want a Long Island."

Angel waved her hand and said, "No, I'm good."

Trina shrugged her shoulders, "Suit yourself." She walked off toward the bar.

Angel laughed, remembering how crazy Trina was. They met when they were in high school and matched each other's crazy. Trina was from a different neighborhood, but she spent a lot of time at Angel's house over the years. As a matter of fact, she was there the night of the accident. She stayed with Angel half the night while the doctors took the glass out. That's why their bond could never be broken.

Angel mixes in with the crowd, dancing to a few old school dances. She was having a good time, until she checked her phone. There were several missed calls from an Unknown number and a few text messages that she knew were from Daniel. She scanned the room, wondering if he had been inside of the party. She knew that if Antwan caught him in the house someone might die. She watched everyone and everything around her.

"Shit," she was startled by a tap on the shoulder. "Girl you scared the hell out of me.

Seeing the look on her face, Carla asked, "Is everything alright?"

"Uh," Angel looked down at her phone, "yeah. Everything is fine."

"You look like you saw a ghost." Carla laughed.

"Nah, I'm good. Everything looks so beautiful, Carla. I'm so happy for you and Antwan."

"Thank you darling. Thank you for coming."

"I wouldn't have missed it for the world." Angel kissed her on the cheek.

The party was still going on and Carla and Antwan stood in front of the room, looking out at all of their guest. Carla seemed to be glowing as he held her by the waist. He kissed her on the cheek and she held her glass up.

"A toast to love." She smiled and then, turned to Antwan. "Baby, you remember how sick I was a few weeks ago?"

"Yeah," he frowned. "Why are you bringing this up now?"

"Baby, I'm pregnant." She said.

"What?" He stared at her for a moment. "You sure? You got a little me up in there?" he felt her stomach.

"Damn baby." He swooped her in his arms and the crowd clapped.

Trina and Angel hugged each other as this was a joyous occasion. Although she and Carla had bumped heads a lot, Trina was happy for her. Angel was excited too but in the back of her mind she was wondering why it couldn't have been her with the baby. Her heart was sad that Daniel had taken life from her. She thought about when they'd found out she was pregnant. That was supposed to be the happiest day of her life, but he was a freaking nightmare.

"Are you okay?" Trina asked her, after a while.

"Yea," Angel wiped away a tear.

Trina wrapped her arm around her shoulder, knowing that she was thinking about her lost child. Angel had been through so much in her life and it hurt Trina to see her going through all of that. She must have felt so alone. Trina tried to make her feel better.

"Ladies?" Jesse walked over to them. "How's the evening going?"

"Good," they both looked at him with a smile.

"So," he touched Trina on the arm, "are you ready to get out of here?" he leaned closer to her. "I have something for you."

"Oh really?" she asked with lit eyes.

They pair climbed into Jesse's BMW and headed toward his apartment. He helped her out of the car and kissed her on the cheek before leading Trina into the house. She sat on the couch and took her shoes off.

"The party was nice, wasn't it?" she asked.

"It was." Jesse sat next to her. "We've been dating for over a year, Trina."

She looked up and smiled at him, "And I love you, baby."

"I know," he smirked. "I love you, too." He said, reaching into his jacket pocket.

"What…" Trina looked at the box and then at him. "You…"

"I want you to be my wife, Katrina Walters." He got on one knee.

"Oh my god!" She snorted like a pig when he opened the box. It was a big ass rock.

If she wasn't loving on him before she definitely was now. She wrapped her arms around his neck and squeezed. "Yes, I'll marry you."

Chapter Sixteen

So, it seemed like everyone was getting their lives together except Angel. She didn't have her man or her baby, but Trina and Carla were living their dream lives. Angel sat at her desk, twirling her hair in her fingers. She looked at her phone, scrolling through social media. She came across a picture of Jesse and Daniel with the caption, Boy's for Life. She frowned knowing that Daniel once had her heart but now she was all alone. She put the phone on the desk face down until it buzzed with a text from Trina.

"Hey girl what's up?" Trina wrote.

"I can't call it." Angel replied.

"Nothing just laying here smiling from ear to ear." Trina admired her engagement ring.

"So, what did Jesse have for you when y'all left the party?" Angel asked.

"Bitch, if I tell you…." Trina sent with a smiling emoji.

"Oh yeah? What is it?"

"Me and Jesse got engaged the other night."

"Wait! What?" Angel sat straight up in her seat.

"Yes, child. That man done went and put a big ass rock on my finger."

"Hold the fuck on, I'ma bout to call your ass." Angel grinned as she hit the telephone icon on her phone.

"Hello?" Angel whispered.

"Yea, girl." Trina was grinning hard.

"Yeah? Let me three-way Carla. Y'all popping out with the shit this week, huh. That one pregnant and you getting engages." Angel clicked over and called Carla.

"I got you on three ways with Trina and you ain't gone believe what this bitch did."

"What?" Carla awaited the juicy news.

"I'm gone let her tell you cause you ain't gone believe this shit." Angel leaned back in her chair.

"What's up, Katrina?"

"Angel trippin cause I told her that me and Jesse got engaged the other night."

"Wait! What?" Carla exclaimed.

"Same thing I said Carla. Like how that is even possible?"

"Come on now y'all act like I'm that shallow. I know a good man when I see one. " Trina said.

Carla laughed. "You are! Didn't you just tell us he wasn't all that in the sack?"

"No that's not what I said." Trina said. "I said, he was decent. I can teach him how to be as freaky as I need him to be." She said as a matter of fact.

"Well, his dick little and now you going to marry him?" Angel laughed.

"Girl, shut up. Everything ain't about sex." Carla tried not to laugh.

Trina whined, "Why can't y'all just be happy for me?"

"Girl, we happy for your bratty ass." Angel and Carla laughed.

"I can hear the bells now." Trina smiled.

"So, which one of us going to be the maid of honor?" Angel asked.

Carla snapped her teeth, "You damn sure know it ain't going to be me. The bitch barely like me."

"You silly as hell. You know I love you." Trina assured her. "Girl, I just got engaged yesterday. I ain't set no date."

"Alright, Hun buns. Let me get back to work." Angel said.

"Talk to y'all later." They hung up.

Chapter Seventeen

Trina rolled out of bed and went downstairs to the den where Jesse was playing the video game. He had a loaded gun on the table and a stack of money next to it. She shook her head but sat down next to him on the couch.

"What you doing?" She asked.

Jesse looked up at her and then back what the TV. "Nothing chilling sitting here playing the game. What's up?"

"Ugh Angel ass getting on my nerves as usual." Trina snapped her teeth.

Jesse started laughing.

"What she do now?"

"It's not so much as what she did. It's what she won't do."

"What you mean?"

Trina shook her head. "Shit with your boy."

"What about him?"

"We getting married, that's your boy and she is my best friend. How we going to have both of them at the wedding?" Trina looked him in the eye.

Jesse put the game controller down and pulled her on his lap. "That's their fight baby. Well you already know you can't tell a grown mutha'fucka what you do. They gone do what they want to. And in her case, she had to leave when she had enough. I don't blame her at all, but Daniel is still my nigga."

"Man, I don't know. You know she got a restraining order against him." Trina reminded him.

"I know that shit wild. I told him the other day he had to chill before somebody gets seriously hurt or worse. He talk about her a lot. I know she pretty and all but what she do to my boy?"

"I swear I be wanting him to say something to me just, so I can have my own reasons to get him fucked up."

"Naw baby stay out of it."

"What? That's my girl what you mean stay out of it?"

"Cause that's my nigga."

"Oh, so you defending him?" She jumped to defense mode.

"If you let me finish. I was saying that's my nigga but if y'all get into it then we gone get into it. Cause I ain't gone let him get reckless with you."

"Oh, okay clean it up then."

"Whatever baby."

Trina shook her head. She wanted both her best friends to be happy, but she knew that Daniel would probably ruin her wedding. For one, he stabbed Twan and two Angel didn't want to be around him. She was in a tough position. Fucking with her, they were going to have a two-person wedding party. She rubbed Jesse's head and kissed him on the forehead.

"Thank you for being so good to me baby." Trina whispered in his ear.

"Humm… how thankful are you?" he put her hand on top of his hardened dick.

She stroked it through his pants and replied, "Very." Then, she pulled it out and slid down in between his legs.

She took it into her mouth, stroking it gently with her tongue. He was moaning and moving around as she deep throated it. He reached behind her and rubbed on her butt. Trina came up for air and stood up in front of him. She put one leg on the table and pushed her panties to the side. Sliding two fingers into her pussy, she watched as Jesse stroked his dick.

"Damn, baby." He said, standing to slid himself inside of her.

Trina leaned her knees on the table while he fucked her from behind. She was moaning and groaning until she reached a sweet orgasm. Jesse smacked her on the ass and sat back on the couch. After catching her breath, she sat down on his dick. She was clawing at his legs while biting on her lip.

"Fuck!" she screeched, climaxing for a second time. "Why you make me cum like this?"

Chapter Eighteen

Thump! Angel heard a loud noise in the front of her house. She sat up in bed and reached for her gun, but it wasn't there. Damn, she remembered that she never took it out of the car.

Thump! The loud noise sounded again. She climbed out of bed, looking for some type of weapon. She snatched the lamp out the wall and went to investigate. As she tiptoed down the hall, she saw a shadow on the wall.

"Fuck," she whispered, nearing the bathroom door.

"Angel," Daniel called out. "I know that you know it's me. You can never hide from me so why don't you just come on home?"

She appeared in front of him. He was sitting on the couch, his hands over his face. She stood there with the lamp in her hand, trying to decide if she wanted to hit him with it.

"Look, you can just go now."

"I want you back, Angel. I am not leaving without you. The restraining order expired days ago. I am allowed to be within 700 feet of you now." He looked up at her with devilish eyes.

"Please," she said, calmly, "just leave."

"I can't leave you, Angel. I love you." He told her, patting the chair. "Come sit with me."

Angel took a deep breath and obliged. She placed the lamp down on the floor next to her and put her hands in her lap. They were sweaty, and her heart was beating fast. She took a deep breath and closed her eyes. "Daniel, why did you hurt me like that?" she found the courage to ask.

"Because I love you. I loved you since the moment I met you. I would never want to love another soul again." He touched her on the face. "You hurt me, too, though, baby." He spoke through tears.

"How? What did I do to you? You took my baby's life."

"Our baby." He put his finger up. "I never meant to do that, but you were too busy running your mouth." He said. "This time…"

"This time?" Angel squinted her eyes. "There is nothing between me and you. After all you've put me through."

"But Angel, I love you." He repeated. "You will be with me because this was all a mistake."

"No, it was you. It was your mistake." Angel stood up. "Leave, Daniel."

He stood up over her. His big buff arms rippling in his shirt. He moved close to her, his cologne clouding the air. She took a deep breath, remembering all of the intimate moments they shared.

"Baby," he touched her chin. "I'm sorry for all of that. Just please give me a second chance." He begged.

"I don't know, Daniel." She was vulnerable.

"Yes, you do. You know that you love me. Couples go through stuff. I was going through something and I have been getting help."

"You have?" Angel looked in his eyes.

He seemed sincere. She wanted to believe that he went and changed his life for her. Her heart was pounding in her chest when he touched her arm. He put his hand under her chin and kissed her on the lips.

"But…" she pulled away. "If I let you back in, back into my life, you have to promise that you will never ever hit me again."

Daniel looked down at her with that beautiful smile she had seen that day in the restaurant and said, "Baby, I promise. I will never hurt you in anyway."

"I love you." She smiled. "I missed you." She kissed him.

He wrapped his arms around her waist, squeezing her tightly. He couldn't believe that his charm had worked on her. He led her down the hall to the bedroom and underdressed her on the bed. It had been months since someone was in her bed, in between her thighs. Angel arched her back and let him kiss her where he missed her. He stroked her pussy so good it was numb. She missed that. She was dancing and moaning to the beat of Daniel's drum. She wanted all of him, deep inside of her love. Call it what you want but a man this good only came around once. He loved her despite of the visible scars all over her body. He loved her way past her pain and if he had to tell it, he loved her to death.

Chapter Nineteen

It had been weeks since Daniel had come back into her life and everything was going well. Daniel had his temper under control and had been going to his meetings and keeping his work on things. Angel was head over heels in love and wouldn't listen to anything about him or against him. At this point they were living together, again, everything was going good so far, they had been getting along and Daniel hasn't raised his voice.

"Thank y'all for coming." Angel opened the door for Carla and Trina.

Carla took her shoes off while saying, "Girl it's been a month since we last saw you. Look at you, gaining weight." She looked at Angel.

Angel blushed and said, "Its cuz I got a man." Angel exclaimed.

"What? Girl are you kidding me?" Carla shook her head and looked at Trina, "I told you she been holding out on us."

"Right, quit acting brand new. You know we got your back even if you don't want to listen," Trina pushed her friend.

"I see Jesse has told you." Angel shrugged.

Carla and Trina both shot her a crazed look. They walked into the apartment and sat on the couch.

"Told us what?" Trina was intrigued.

"That me and Daniel…"

"Hold the hell up," Carla threw her hands up. "Your name and his name don't even belong in the same sentence. I know dog on well y'all ain't back together!"

"Lower your voice," Angel looked over her shoulder.

"The nigga here?" Trina's eyes got big. "Yo Angel, you really tripping. I ain't with this here shit. It's your life and my man said stay out of it." She stood up, grabbing her purse.

"You're leaving?"

"Yes, girl I love you but that man," she pointed down the hall, "he don't. He don't give a damn if you live or die."

Carla stood up too, holding her baby bump. "I'm with Trina on this one." She shook her head.

The two of them left and Angel sat on the couch, sobbing. Then, Daniel came from the bedroom with a towel wrapped around his waist.

"I take it your friends still aren't too fond of me, are they?" he smirked, sitting down next to her.

"No, they remember what you did to me. How can they forget? Could you?" Angel stood up and went into the kitchen where he followed her.

She opened the fridge and took out the juice.

"I do remember Angel and I keep apologizing." Daniel grabbed her arm and he kissed her lips "But if them hoes won't respect me, they're no longer welcomed."

"Wait! What does that mean?" Angel frowned.

Daniel let her go and took a step back. "Just what I said; if they got a problem with me then they can't come over my house."

"You mean our house, right?"

"Angel look I said what I meant, and I meant what I said." Daniel back tracked out of the kitchen.

She folded her arms across her chest. Even though he hadn't hit her, he was still arrogant. She didn't want to rebuttal out of fear that he might beat the crap out of her. She knew that Carla and Trina would never approve of their relationship. The only way they would ever be as cool as they once were being if they never saw Daniel or talked about him.

Chapter Twenty

A few weeks later, Angel met with Carla and Trina at the bridal shop to get fitted for Trina's wedding. She sat quietly while they tried on different dresses. She didn't want to seem rude, but she wasn't feeling like herself. She watched them through a big pair of shades.

"Angel!" Trina twirled around a in a dress. "Isn't this beautiful?"

"Angel?" Carla calmed down and sat on the chair next to her. "Are you okay, girl?"

"Yeah?" Trina touched her cold hands. "What's the matter Angel?"

Angel looked at her friends and said, "I can't stay long Daniel's expecting dinner by the time he gets home."

Carla looked at her closely she sits down. She reached over the table to remove her sunglasses then sat back down shaking her head.

"Angel?" Carla held her stomach.

"What? It's not that bad." Angel looked between the two of them.

Trina snapped her teeth and sat at Angel's feet, "Not that bad? Have you seen yourself?"

"Yes, I have." Angel retorted as she snatched her glasses and put them back on. "Come on y'all that's not what I came here for. I just wanted to hang out with my girls for a little bit."

"That seems like all we get to do anyway. Is hang for a bit like he got you on a leash or something."

Trina was sick and tired of Angel making excuses for him. She left him only to go right back. It was a phenomenon that no one could ever understand. Domestic violence was claiming so many lives, especially in the African American Community. Countless men and women are killed each year at the hands of someone who was supposed to love them. It's being swept under the rug and called incidents of passion. Trina had a bad feeling that none of this was going to end well. She feared for her friend's life.

"Come on, Trina, it's not even like that." Angel huffed.

"You sound like him now." Carla shook her head.

"Well tell us how it is then Angel." Trina rolled her eyes. "You tripping and falling on this nigga fist? I mean just tell me something. What is it that keeps you going back?"

"So y'all just gone gang up on me? No one loves me! Who is going love me? I have forty little gashes on my body. I watched my mother die. Who is going to want me? That man he loves me. All of me and he don't care about my past"

"Angel, he doesn't love you." A tear fell from Carla's eye.

"That's where you're wrong. He does love me." Angel assured. "He has to love me. He took me back after I had a restraining order out on him. I brought a gun and swore I would shot him if he ever came near me." Angel cried.

"Honey that's not love. Love doesn't hurt, and it doesn't turn you against your friends and the people that really love you."

"Yeah, Angel, he ain't no good for you." Carla shook her head.

"Now I came here to spend some time with my girls but y'all want to judge me." Angel stuffed her scarf in her purse and snatched her phone off the table. "Have fun." She pulled her purse on her should.

"Angel wait!" Carla went after her. "Please don't go back there."

"I have to get my man's dinner ready," Angel huffed as she brushed past them.

First, she stopped at the grocery store. She knew that the girls were only looking out for her best interest, but she was not about to let them talk bad about her or her man.

Daniel was good to her and he took care of her better than a man ever have. As soon as she walked in the house with groceries Daniel greeted her at the door.

"Hey baby," She reached up to kiss him, but he moved away.

"What's up? Where you been?" he asked, closing the door.

Angel carried the bags into the kitchen and sat them down on the counter. "I'm so sorry I'm late. I was out with Trina and Carla. I'm about to get dinner started right now."

Daniel was putting on his sneakers, hardly paying her any mind. He was thinking about the move he had to bust with Jesse. There was money to be made and she was telling him an excuse about why he hadn't eaten dinner. He shook his head, wanting to smack the hell out of her. He didn't though.

"Oh no rush I'm bout to go. I'll grab something to eat while I'm out," he kissed her on the cheek and left.

"Now here it is I'm rushing from spending time with my friends to come home and make dinner and you leave?" Angel felt underappreciated. She started to put the groceries in the refrigerator as he walked out of the door.

Selfish ass. She slammed the cabinets closed. "I can't stand his ass."

Why in the hell is Angel still with his clown ass? Come on, when will she ever get a grip. From the outside looking in, he was a piece of shit who didn't give to damns about her. She didn't know it though. She was blinded by money and bling. Hell, if you asked her, she deserved it. Angel was one of millions of girls who thought they could change a man. If she did whatever he wanted he wouldn't treat her so bad. She thought that she could make him an honest man one day and she hoped that he would learn that he didn't have to beat her for her to get her to love him back.

Angel tried waiting up for him before going to bed but

he had been gone for hours with no return phone call. When Daniel first came home he jumped straight in the shower and into the bed. Angel tried cuddling up with him, but his body language told her otherwise. She reached to play with his dick, but he pushed her hand away.

"Come on I'm tired." Daniel told her.

"Tired?" Angel huffed as she rolled over with an attitude. She decided to get up and check his pockets as to where he's been. She picked his phone up and started scrolling through. There was a familiar number that she had seen numerous times before. As she continued to scroll she clicked on his messages and her eyes got big. She couldn't believe what she was reading she started crying holding the phone in her hand.

"Oh my God! I can't believe this. I just really can't believe this. After all that I've done for you?" Angel cried as she pointed to Daniel while he was sleep. "All the shit I put up with from you, but you love her? You love her?" She started getting louder.

Daniel had rolled over and she got nervous, so she put the phone behind her back. She scrolled down some more and found a picture of Daniel and the female. He was hugged up with the same bitch that came to the door in Vegas. He told her that was over. Angel had ready played the fool for too damn long.

"I can't believe this," Angel gasped as she put the phone back in his pants.

She started pacing the floor thinking of things he had done to her. "I should kill him in his sleep" as she thought about everything he had put her through. I should shoot this stupid nigga. She went to her bag in search of her gun. She couldn't find it in the bag.

"Where is my shit?" she looked around the room but couldn't find the gun.

I'm tripping, she thought as she laid down in bed.

Chapter Twenty- One

Daniel pulled her closer and wanted to cuddle, she just laid there frowning. The very next day Daniel got up and left without so much as a good morning to Angel. Things were finally starting to take a toll on Angel. She was getting tired.

"Hello." Angel said when Carla answered the phone.

Her mind was racing, and she really needed to get the fuck away from Daniel. I got a feeling, she bit her bottom lip.

"Hey girl what's up?"

"Nothing just got up."

Carla took a deep breath. "Angel listen I didn't call to argue with you but I gotta tell you something."

"I'm listening." Angel tapped her foot.

"Look at that picture I just sent to you and tell me if you recognize her." Carla waited.

Angel took the phone off her ear and opened up Carla's message and was in shock.

"Yes, that's the stripper from Vegas." Angel remembered all the pictures she had saw in his phone. "This nigga…"

"I just seen her and Daniel leaving Coney Island." Carla blurted out.

"Ooh I'm gone fuck him up." Angel said aloud but knew there was no truth to it. There was no way she would win a fight with Daniel, he might just kill her this time.

"Wait Angel there's more," Carla paused as she braced herself for what was coming next.

"What? What else could there be?" Angel snapped her teeth.

"She's pregnant."

"Pregnant?" Angel screeched as she held her stomach thinking about the miscarriage she suffered. "Are you sure she's pregnant?"

"Yup look at the other picture I just sent."

"This can't be his baby. No this is just too much." Angel shook her head as tears started to fall.

"Calm down. I'm sorry you had to find out like this, but it was best you know."

"I just can't believe this there has to be some type of explanation."

"Explanation? Angel the proof is in the pictures."

"Carla that's not really telling me nothing. I mean yeah he's standing with her but that doesn't actually me it's his baby."

Carla slaps herself in the forehead. How can this girl be this dumb? Is she listening to herself right now? Like come on, seriously.

"You confirmed it's the chick from Vegas. She's pregnant seen with your man and you don't see nothing wrong with that?"

"I mean yeah I do but I trust him."

Carla eyes got big. "Honestly if he did something stupid fucked around and got her pregnant I mean I wouldn't leave."

"You wouldn't leave? If that was his baby?"

"No! The baby has nothing to do with it. I love him, and we will work it out."

"Angel I don't understand you. How can you keep allowing him to hurt you?"

"Carla, I appreciate you telling me this but it's fine I'll handle it." Carla was so disappointed that she just hung up the phone.

They have been friends since high school she couldn't believe Angel was letting a man get between them. As the night went by Daniel returned home to see Angel sleep on the couch. He took her phone out her hands and went through it. He came across the pictures that Carla had sent and got furious. He snatched the covers off of Angel so hard causing her to wake up. As soon as her eyes were fully focused she saw his hands getting closer. He grabbed her by her arms and started yanking her back and forth.

"So, you got your little bitches following me huh?" Daniel growled in her face.

Angel squinted. "What are you talking about?"

"Don't lie to me," He smacked her in the face.

"I'm not lying Daniel I promise."

"So, you ain't got these mutha'fuckas following me? Taking pictures of me?"

Daniel was cursing and screaming at her, chasing her from one end of the couch to the other. She used her hands to block her face, in case he decided to smack her again. He was yelling about the pictures and the girl. She heard him say that she was having his baby. Angel felt worthless. Another woman was having his baby, but he killed theirs. She cried for the life she lost as she tried to get away from him.

"I swear I don't." she cried.

"Then what the fuck is this?" He shoved the phone in her face. Angel tried to catch her breath.

"Carla sent me these. She said she was trying to look out and protect me."

"Well let's see if she can protect you now!" Daniel yelled as he punched her in the mouth.

He pulled her by her feet and threw her on the floor and began kicking her. He stomped her as she tried covering her head, so he wouldn't kick her in the face again. Angel screamed and yelled, kicking to get away from him. She crawled across the floor and he grabbed her by the ankles again.

"Please, Daniel." She cried, kicking him in the stomach.

He doubled over and glared at her while he tried to catch his breath. It was the first time in a while that she tried to fight him back. She thought about the night that he stomped her until their baby died.

"You son of a bitch!" she screeched, jumping to her feet. "You got this bitch pregnant? Huh?" she smacked him. "You in here kicking my ass but you got a bitch pregnant?" she hit him again. He lunged at her, knocking her back on the floor.

"The fuck wrong with you!?" he yelled, pouncing on her face.

"I'm sorry please don't hit me no more." She cried out in pain, her face covered in blood from the beating.

"Tell your friend to stay the fuck out my business. They don't know what the fuck their talking about."

"Okay."

"Sending you this bullshit got you in the middle of all this drama."

"I didn't believe her baby," Angel cried as she held onto his leg crying and shaking.

"Matter of fact distance yourself from them. I don't even want you talking to them bitches no more."

"Alright."

"Do you understand me?" as he pulled her hair.

"Yes!" she cried out as he pushed her head off him.

"Get up and go clean yourself up."

Angel got up off the floor holding her side. Daniel had kicked her repeatedly out of anger. She stumbled to the bathroom and looked in the mirror. Her hair was all over her head she was bleeding from her nose and her lips her. Her eye was slightly closed with a big bruise already forming. Her jaw was swollen, and she have fingerprints on her neck from being choked by him. She tried to pull it together without breaking down and seeing herself. When she want to straighten the living room the chair was knocked over, the couch cushions were thrown all over the floor. It just looked a mess. She couldn't believe it the man she loved had done it to her again. As she continued cleaning up the living room Daniel came out to her pulling her closer.

"You know I love you right?"

"Yes."

"I'm sorry I'll never put my hands you again. I promise."

Even though he had gone back on his word several times before he had a way of making her believe him. She felt humiliated that her friends had insight on her relationship. They knew how low-down Daniel really was. She was embarrassed that her man was out wining and dining a girl that was pregnant with his child. She was scared that he had the power to make her feel worthless.

She slowly turned on the shower and placed a towel on the back of the toilet seat. Daniel was standing there, watching as she peeled her clothes off, revealing all of the scars and bruises on her body. She was covered in black and blue marks. Her hair was clinging to her face and the blood was still seeping through.

"Baby," Daniel spoke to her in a soft voice, "I promise to make it up to you."

Angel nodded her head and stepped into the piping hot water. She let it cascade down on her sore limbs as tears of sorrow and guilt rolled down her swollen cheeks. The water poured over her head and washed away the blood. She knew that she would die loving Daniel, but she hoped that it was no time soon. She closed her eyes, imagining being reunited with her mother and suddenly, noise come from her mouth. She wept with the overwhelming feeling that none of this was going to end well.

Chapter Twenty-Two

The sun crept into the room, awakening Angel from a slumber. She rolled over to find a bouquet of flowers in Daniel's spot. There was a note and a small box. She opened it to find a pair of diamond earrings. Placing them back on the bed, she pulled the sheets back and pulled her feet to the side of the bed. Her face hurt all over and feeling her lip she knew that it was swollen. She took a sip of water and then, went into the bathroom.

The sight was one that she had seen before; a black eye and a busted nose. Angel was utterly disgusted at the person who was staring back at her. She took a cloth and gently wiped her face. The bathroom door creaked, and she turned to see Daniel staring at her.

"I look hideous," she proclaimed.

"You good?" He asked peeking his head in the bathroom.

She turned to look at him, "Yeah I'm good."

"Okay now that's my girl. You don't have any plans for today?" he acted as if he hadn't just whopped her ass like they were in a WWF match.

"No." Angel sighed, "Besides I can't go outside looking like this."

"Why not? You look beautiful. Any man would be lucky to have you by his side."

She couldn't believe he was praising her after what he did but that just showed her how much he really loved her. She smiled, stilling looking at her battered face in the mirror.

"You really mean that?"

"Would I lie to you?" he asked, nonchalantly.

Angel pondered the question for a moment and clenched her teeth. Yes, she thought, you would lie to me. You've been lying to me all along. She wanted to tell him how she really felt but she knew that it would result in an ass whopping. She was too exhausted to fight with him.

So, she smiled, nervously, and said, "No you wouldn't."

He kissed her forehead and patted her on the butt. "Finish getting yourself together. I'm going to holla at Jesse for a minute." He told her, closing the door.

She stood there looking in the mirror for a few more minutes before looking for her phone. She scrolled back to the picture Carla has sent her and just cried for about an hour. She went downstairs to the kitchen and pulled out a bottle of vodka. She poured a half glass and took it back without a chaser. She was angry with herself. She didn't deserve any of this. She turned up the radio as loud as it would go, trying to drown out the pain.

"What is wrong with me? Why can't I keep him happy? Why does he need to go to her? When he has me right here." She screamed on top of the bass of the music. "I can't take this shit!"

Searching the medicine cabinet, she found a bottle of Percocet's that Daniel had been using for his leg. Hastily she opened the bottle and poured a few into her hand. It was to numb the pain—she swallowed several of the pilled. Someone was calling her phone and it kept interrupting the music.

"Go away!" Angel yelled, smacking herself on the head. "Please just leave me alone!"

The phone wouldn't stop ringing though. "Oh my god!" she screeched, picking it up. "What do you want?" she yelled at the caller.

"Hello?" Carla was concerned. "Hello, Angel?"

"What?" Angel asked angrily. "Why won't everyone just leave me alone?"

"I was just calling to check on you."

"Check on me? My man beat me like Holifield because of you and now you wanna check on me?" Angel cried. "You don't care about me. You don't love me. You know what? Don't even come to my funeral." Angel shouted.

"Funeral?" Carla looked at the phone. "What are you talking about?

"I'm going to…"

"Hello? Angel?" Carla panicked. "Oh my god! Antwan!" she yelled, hopping off the couch.

"Where you going baby?" He asked.

"Somethings wrong with Angel." She told him, grabbing her purse.

"But your doctor said you need to get some rest." He was concerned for his wife.

Carla kissed him on the cheek and said, "Baby I will be fine I have to go check on my girl."

Carla wobbled out of the door and called Trina as she got into the car. She was in such a frenzy that she couldn't explain what was going on. Her breathing as heavy and her mind was racing. All she could really tell Trina was that something was amiss and that they needed to get to Daniel's house. She hung up the phone and tossed it in the passenger seat, running red lights to get to Angel.

Please, Carla prayed as she neared Daniel's block, please Lord let her be okay. Tears streamed down her face as her car met Trina's in front of Daniel's house. She climbed out and called the police as they went to bang on the door.

"Angel!" Trina and Carla yelled, trying to get a good look inside.

"Where are the police?" Trina looked around.

She bone rushed the door but couldn't get it opened. Then, a squad car pulled up.

"Ma'am," one of the officers said, "what seems to be the problem?"

"I was on the phone with my friend. She sounded erratic and then just stopped talking mid-sentence. I think she's hurt." Carla held her belly as she spoke to the officer. "Please. Help her."

"Ma'am we're going to knock and try to get her to come

out, something called a wellness check." He explained. "Please come off the porch and wait down here." The officer pointed.

Trina and Carla frowned but obliged. The officers knocked on the door and rang the doorbell to no avail. One of them decided to check around back.

"She's in there, lying on the floor." He ran back.

"Oh my god!" Carla rubbed her temple as the officers used force to open the door.

She and Trina ran into the house where Angel was laying, practically lifeless on the kitchen floor. There was a half empty bottle of Vodka on the counter and an empty bottle of pills. The officer checked her pulse.

"There's a slight pulse. Call for a bus."

"Yes," the other officer pressed his walkie talkie. "We need an ambulance to 224 Mercer Ave."

A few minutes later, an ambulance arrived. By then, neighbors were starting to gather outside. They were whispering about all the noise they had been hearing in the past few weeks. None of them thought to call the police. Carla shook her head as the EMT's brought Angel out on the stretcher. Her face was beat badly and she was hardly breathing. They loaded her into the back of the ambulance with Trina and Carla in tow.

"I'm here baby just breathe, breathe Angel." Trina held her hand. "I'm so sorry." She whispered, kissing her on the cheek.

She sat down next to Carla, holding her hand too. Carla was trying to keep calm because she was supposed to be on bedrest. She texted Antwan and told him to meet them at the hospital. It was unclear if Angel was going to survive. Tears were rolling from both Trina and Carla's eyes as the ambulance stopped in front of the emergency room doors. There were already two doctors waiting to pump Angel's stomach. They watched, helplessly, as they hauled her off.

"Oh my God! Did you see her?" Trina gasped as they sat down in the waiting room.

"Yes, but we gotta have faith. We serve a higher God," Carla prayed.

"But Carla she wasn't breathing. Why? Why didn't I check up on her more often? I could have called or came by." Trina rubbed her palms on her pants. "I was too busy getting ready for the wedding."

"Trina don't beat yourself up. It's not your fault Angel will pull through this trust me. I feel just as bad as you, but she's strong." Carla put her hand on top of Trina's.

They sat there for almost an hour, waiting on the doctor to tell them something about their friend. Carla got a little hungry, so she and Antwan walked down to the hall to the vending machines. Trina was pacing back and forth when she heard a familiar voice.

"What's going on in here?" Daniel asked.

Trina turned around and looked at him with fire in her eyes. It was taking everything in her not to pull out her shank and stab his ass like he had done Twan in the club. He walked toward her, and she backed up.

"You need to leave." She said through clenched teeth.

"Nah, what's up?" he asked. "Where's Angel? People calling me talking about the cops and shit at my crib. Where she at?" he snarled.

"Man, go head. You need to leave. You ain't bout to do no more than you already done." Trina told him.

Daniel clenched his teeth and grabbed her by the arm. She looked up at him and then, down at his hand on her arm. "Please don't get me fucked up, I ain't Angel." She said as a matter of fact.

He shoved her and said, "What happened?"

"You know exactly what happened. You left her there after you beat her ass." Trina yelled in her face.

Hearing Trina's booming voice, Carla knew that Daniel must have been there. She looked at Twan who shook his head.

"Baby walk behind me cuz if this fool act reckless, I'm going to kill him." Twan told her.

Carla and Antwan proceeded back down the hall. Daniel was all in Trina's face, asking her about Angel. She told him again that he had to leave but he wasn't listening. Antwan slowly approached and cleared his throat. Daniel turned around, sizing him up.

"What's up, my boy?" Antwan asked, his arms spread in front of him. "The lady asked you to leave."

Daniel chuckled, "The fuck you is? They body guard?"

"Man, look. I'ma need you to go," Antwan pointed over his shoulder, "quietly."

"Nigga, I don't know what kind of…"

Then, a doctor approached them. He cleared his throat and they all stopped to look at him. He introduced himself and then said, "Thank God you all found her when you did. She's going to be okay." He smiled.

Carla and Trina were relieved and hugged each other with the good news. Daniel sat down and put his head in his hands. He was rocking back and forth as if any of them would have sympathy for him. Trina rolled her eyes thinking that he was an attention seeking nigga. She brushed past him and followed Carla to Angel's room.

They both leaned on either side of the bed, kissing her on the cheek. She was grateful that they had come to her rescue. She had an epiphany as she laid there, dying. She was through with Daniel. There was no turning back from this. Though she had tried before she knew now that her life was worth much more than he was willing to give her. She cried, knowing that her friends really loved her. As they stood there, Daniel was brave enough to walk into the room. Trina stared at him with a clenched jaw.

"What's up?" he looked at Angel.

"Nothing baby we were just talking." She said, shyly.

"Yeah Daniel we were just talking. Is there a problem?" Carla rolled her eyes.

"Naw ain't no problem just checking on my girl." Daniel touched her leg.

"Your girl is doing fine no thanks to you." Trina snapped.

Daniel glared at her. "And what's that supposed to mean?"

"It means that your days of beating her are over." Trina retorted as Trina stood from her seat.

"I don't know what you're talking about," Daniel shrugged as he looked at Angel. "Baby do I beat you?" He stared at her, putting fear in her heart.

Angel was quiet for a moment and then she swallowed hard and said, "Yes, you beat me, and I am sick and tired of it."

Daniel backed up, balling up his fist. "Aight, you wanna play?" he asked.

"Daniel, it's over." Angel cried. "I'm not dealing with this anymore."

"You're my woman. You belong to me!" he shouted.

Trina stepped up to him and held on tight to her purse. She would have zapped his ass if she had to. "I suggest you get your ass out of here." She waved. "I ain't scared of you."

Daniel snickered, "Yeah okay. You ain't supposed to be scared of me."

"I'm glad you know it," Trina snapped her teeth as Trina walked up in his face.

"Trina, he ain't even worth it," Carla held her by the arm.

"Both of y'all tripping must be that time of the month. I'll see you later on baby" Daniel said as he back out of the room.

As he left Carla frowned at him the whole way out then closed the door. Carla took a seat and Trina held Angel's hand.

"I can't believe you keep letting this nigga get to you." She shook her head.

"Not now Trina." Angel glared up at her. "I'm serious this time, I'm leaving."

"What does he have over you? I mean is the dick that good? This nigga can do whatever he wants to you and it's okay." Trina gets all emotionally upset and sat down in the chair and stared out the window.

"Trina," as she took a deep breath "I'm not as strong as y'all."

"Yes, you are," Carla grabbed her hand.

"Let me finish. Y'all have people in y'all lives that make you feel special and give you all the love y'all need physically I don't. Well I didn't until I met Daniel. I know he has his faults but he's not completely the blame. I played a role in this. I let him do all the stuff he did. I was searching for something." Angel told them.

"Bullshit." Trina shook her head. "Now I feel you wanting to be with someone who loves you but fuck that nigga Daniel he don't love you."

"He says he does." Angel looked down. "I heard that sorry shit before though."

"Angel love doesn't hit you. Love won't keep you away from the people that love you most and in your case his love baby girl love will get you killed. Angel look at where you're at."

"He didn't put me here. I took those pills myself." Angel glared at Carla.

"Ok so he didn't force feed you the pills, but he might as well have had." Trina said.

"I took them because I just felt overwhelmed with stuff." Trina got a mirror out of her purse and put it in her face.

"Look at yourself. Is this the love you want? He made

you lose your child for God sakes. What more does he need to do to you before you really he will kill you?"

"We definitely don't want to see you dead."

"Definitely."

"I don't have anywhere to go." Angel whispered.

"Now see that's where you're wrong. You can stay with me."

"I'm so scared. He gets so mad out of the blue at me and before I know it we're fighting. I don't know what to do now."

"Well first and foremost you need to make a police report and get a restraining order against him."

"Again? It didn't work the first time, obviously." Angel shook her head.

"Because then, you thought you needed him. You don't know."

"Trina you don't understand. The last time he told me if I ever tried to leave him he would kill me, and I believe him."

"And so, do we. That's why you're not going back to live with him."

"Exactly! Cause seeing you on that floor did it for me. Your life is worth more than what you know."

"I feel like such a fool." Angel mumbled as she cried with her hands over her face. Carla got up to sit on the edge of the bed. She wrapped her arms around her.

"No sweetie you're not a fool. You have nothing to feel ashamed about. We all go through things in life. You're not the first one to go through this and surely you won't be the last. But I promise you that he won't hurt you again."

"I can't believe y'all are still here after the way I treated y'all."

"You can't get rid of us that easy. Sticks and stones may break our bones, but words will never hurt us."

"He's gone be pissed when he finds out I'm getting discharged today."

"He will he be alright."

"He ain't got no choice but to be alright. Cause if he come to my mother fuckin house with that bullshit I'm telling you he ain't leaving."

Chapter Twenty-Three

After Angel was discharged the ladies made it to Trina's and helped her get settled in. Angel appreciated all that they were doing. Daniel had her shutting out the only family she had. Carla was getting ready to burst and Trina was still planning her wedding, but they found it in their hearts to make time to help her through the storm.

She sat down on the edge of the bed and smiled.

"Trina thank you for letting me stay here."

Trina put a few items on the dresser and replied, "Girl I ain't trippin."

"Angel, I'll bring you a few outfits by tomorrow, so you have a change of clothes." Carla told her. "If I don't pop by then."

"Girl, as big as that belly is. My niece said she on her way." Trina laughed.

"Your niece? You're my friend this week, huh?" Carla laughed.

Trina shook her head. "I think you be trying to sneak diss on the low with that shit. I don't know how many times I got to tell you, I love you like a fat kid love cake."

"Damn," Angel snapped her teeth, "all my stuff is at Daniel's house, this so fucked up."

"Material shit that's all. It can be replaced."

"I'm just saying! I can't believe I got myself in this situation. I mean I can see if I had to just spend the night or maybe even the weekend, but I'm basically needed to live here with nothing to my name." Her voice started to crack.

"Angel as long as you got us we got you're back. You act like it's the end of the world it's a break up. You know with every break up there's always things that get caught up in the middle like a custody battle," she laughs. "It is just a minor setback that's all. You'll bounce back" they start laughing.

"Thanks Carla you always make me see the light at the

end of the tunnel." Angel smiled.

"Just don't go in it," they laughed. Something was still bothering Carla and she needed to know. So, she jumped straight to the questions. "Why did you go back to him after you were turning over a new leaf?"

"I missed him, and he seemed genuine when he apologized. I thought he was changing. I believe in second chances. I mean we've been going through this for a while now. We were all hanging out and he had got mad at me for something. I don't even remember what it was. But we were all sitting down then Daniel walked over to me and poured the whole bottle of champagne on me."

"You gotta be kidding me."

"Nope. I kid you not. It didn't matter where we were or who was around if he wanted to do something to me he would just do it. He didn't care. I was so embarrassed."

"Ok let me ask you a question. Why you ain't say nothing or fight back?"

"Because I loved him. And even though that's not a good enough reason at the time I thought it was. I was scared. I mean cause just look at me and look at him it wasn't too much I could do with him. His temper was strong enough for three men. I just tried to steer clear."

"I'm just glad that you've finally had enough." Trina interrupted.

"Yeah it's embarrassing too. Cause at the same time you looking for that shoulder to lean on or ear to talk to but not wanting to look stupid cause you're still with him, so you keep it bottled in."

"I wish I could have done something sooner." Trina shook her head. "But that's my man's boy."

"Well we're going to let you lay down and get you some rest. And ill check on you tomorrow."

"Thanks Carla." Angel touched her hand with a smile.

"Yeah I'll be right out here too if you need me."

"Thanks Trina."

She turned the TV off and as soon as Angel laid down she started to drift asleep. Then her phone started ringing.

"Hello." She answered, groggily.

"Hey baby. What's going on?" Daniel's voice came through the phone.

"Nothing just laying here." She half lied.

"Yeah I'll be up there to get you in the morning. I would've came back up there today but I ain't feel like dealing with your friends. I told you I didn't want to hang around and bitter bitches anyway always hating."

"Hating?" Angel sat up in the bed. "No one want this shit you call love, Daniel."

"What? Is you stupid? You gotta man who loves you and will do anything for you."

"I do?" Angel shook her head. "You don't love me boy. I told you it was over."

"What? What the hell you mean do you? Man, I'll smack the shit out of your ungrateful ass. See that's the shit I'm talking about Angel. You get with your little friends and start acting brand-new. I told your ass the only way you leaving me is in a body bag and I mean that shit." He spat.

"Don't call me no more!" Angel screamed into the phone.

"See that's the shit I'm talking about. I'm just gone hang up now before you piss me off. I'll just see you tomorrow" Before she could get another word in he hung up on her, so she went to sleep.

The next day Angel's phone was ringing nonstop with each call being sent to voicemail. Daniel was blowing her phone up trying to find her. She got tired of him calling and decided to answer it.

"Hello."

"Oh, your ass wanna answer now? Huh? Where the hell you at?"

"I got discharged."

"I know that smart ass. But that ain't telling me where you at."

"You're never going to find out where I am. It's o-v-e-r!" she shouted.

"Man, listen. Bring your rabbit ass home. You don't do shit. You don't work, and you don't go to school. Who going to take care of your spoiled ass? "

"Whatever." Angel pressed end on her phone. He called right back.

He called continuously for the next ten minutes, leaving voicemails and text. He was threatening her, saying that he will kill her when he caught her. She closed her eyes and set up with her head down on her knees. He just kept calling back to back. Trina came in living room and noticed Angel with her knees bent on the couch and her face buried.

"What's wrong?" Angel jumped up. wiping her face. "I didn't hear you walk in the room."

"What's wrong? Is Daniel calling?" Trina sat next to her. Angel wouldn't even look at her. "Is he?"

"Yes nonstop," Angel cried, showing her the buzzed phone.

"Let me answer it. Give it here" Trina frowned and she gestured for her to hand her the phone.

"Hello?" Trina waited for him to respond.

"Bitch you got one more time…" Trina interrupts

"Sorry but there are no bitches here."

"Put my girl on the phone please."

"First of all, she ain't your girl. Now quit calling this fucking phone."

Daniel snapped, "Now y'all playing games and I ain't the one to play with."

"Daniel all that you blowing out your mouth might scare the next one but not this one." Trina said with her hand on her hip.

"Just put Angel on the phone." He huffed.

"She'll call you back" Trina lied and hung up. But as soon as she handed Angel the phone it rung again.

"He is really starting to get on my nerves." Trina wanted to launch the phone across the room.

"Mine too and he ain't even my man. Look just quit answering his phone calls that's all."

"I'm bout to in fact I'm going to put his ass on the reject list."

"Good. Shit that nigga is crazy anyway stop fucking with him. No calls, text nothing."

Angel shook her head. "Easier said than done. I know that."

"Not overnight of course not. it's going to take one day at a time and more than one."

"I love you." Angel reached for a hug.

"I love you too girl. I'm about to go get my nails done you wanna roll?"

"Naw I'm just gone chill here."

"Alright but don't be soaking my pillows with your tears." Trina joked. as Angel smiled at her. "That's right smile through the pain. Don't give him no more power over you."

"I'm not." Angel sighed.

"Okay see you in a bit," Trina told her as she closed the door behind her. A

s Trina got in her car and pulled off Daniel pulled up. He got out the car looking around before heading up the stairs. He knocked on the door covering up the peephole.

"Angel, it's me. Baby I know you're in there. Open up so we can talk." Daniel shouted.

"How did you find me Daniel?" Angel questioned as she covered her mouth with her hand.

"All that don't matter baby. Open the door I just wanna talk."

"I'll call you later Daniel I promise," she stuttered.

"Naw you ain't gotta do all that I'm right here. Open the

door." He insisted.

"Daniel."

"Angel open the fuckin door before I break it down. And you ain't gone like." He started banging.

As terrified as she was she opened it. He walked in looked her right in the face and punched her. Angel fell back on the couch, holding her face. She looked up at him with tears in her eyes.

"Aw, baby. Don't cry." He whispered, pulling a tissue out of his pocket. "My lady shouldn't be crying."

"Please," she begged.

"It's so good to see you baby," He lifted her chin up and kissed her. "What are you crying for? You should be happy to see me. I thought I would never see you again." She tried scooting over on the couch near her phone, but Daniel pulled her closer. "Aren't you happy to see me?"

"Yes." She nodded.

Daniel put his hand on her hip. "Why you ain't actin like it?"

"How you want me to act? I'm happy you're here." She lied.

"Prove it."

"Prove it how?" He unzipped his pants and pulled out his dick.

"Suck it," she looked down then back up to him.

"No what if Trina comes back home?"

"Shit she can get some too. That bitch talk too much she need a mouthful." He put his hand on her head and pushed it down on his lap. She put the tip in her mouth and started crying. He grabbed her by the hair and forced it in her mouth. She was sobbing and crying trying to get up, but he wouldn't let her. So, she did the only thing that she could do to get up. She bit him and jumped up wiping her mouth.

"I'm sorry. I couldn't breathe you was choking me. I'm sorry," she was balled up at the end of the couch. Daniel got up holding his dick in his hand.

"So, you want to bite me bitch?"

"I said I was sorry Daniel please." She tried to push him away.

"Please what?" Daniel cocked back his hand as he punched her in the face repeatedly. Her face was starting to swell blood was coming from her nose and mouth. After continuing to take the blows her eye was damn near shut. When he let her go her little body just fell to the floor. She laid there motionless. He slapped her hard to wake her up then he picked her limp body up and started choking her till her face was turning blue. He got up and sat down on the couch and just watched her.

"Hello?" Trina answered Jesse's call.

"Aye Trina where you at?"

"At the nail shop getting my nails done. What's up?'

"Is Angel with you?" He sounding worried.

"Naw she's at the house. Why? What's going on?"

"This nigga Daniel talking about finding her."

"Man, if he don't go somewhere. Damn!"

"Yeah that nigga tripping. That's my boy and all but I ain't down with all that shit he talking."

"Like what?"

"Talking bout if she ain't gone be with him she ain't gone be with nobody. Shit like that."

"That nigga need to gone bout his business cause it's a wrap."

"I said that the last time they got into it. That nigga on some other shit."

"Hold on I'm bout to call her." Trina said as she clicked over to call her the phone just rang for a while bout five or six times. The went to voicemail so she tried dialing her again and got the voicemail. "Hello."

"Did you get her?"

"Naw now she making me nervous. Cause I don't know if she straight or just didn't hear it or if he over there. Naw fuck that I ain't taking no chances. I'm following my first mind. Can you meet me there just in case that mutha'fucka over there?"

"Yeah I got you I'm on my way."

Trina cuts mani and pedi short and told them she had an emergency and had to leave. She's a regular so they knew she would be back. Trina jumped in her car and stabbed off. She pulled out her phone to call Angel again but kept getting the voicemail.

"I hope she's just sleep or something or can't hear the phone. Cause I'm telling you if that nigga is over at my house with that bullshit I'm going to jail."

She continued to drive fast speeding through traffic. She put her hazards on so people would know something was wrong and to get out of her way. Jesse had pulled up p to the house first and knew that he had beat Trina there. He go out his car and was about to call and let Trina know he was there until he heard screams coming from her house. So, he just headed up to her flat. He pushed open the door and noticed Daniel standing over Angel pulling her hair pointing gun in her face.

"Daniel?" he shouted looking over at Angel crying hysterically.

"Jesse man what's up?" Daniel looked deranged.

"What the fuck you doing?" Jesse asked as he gestures his hand at the situation.

"Aww man I ain't gone shoot this bitch. I'm just letting her know she ain't going nowhere." Daniel waved the gun in the air.

"Jesse please help me," Angel cried out.

Daniel pulled her hair tighter and pressed the gun to her face. "Shut the fuck up. You only speak when I tell you too. Stupid ass bitch!"

Jesse pushed Trina out the door and stepped into the living room. He was going to try his best to talk the nigga down, but the way Daniel had been acting lately there were only a few ways this could go.

"Daniel nigga put the gun down before that shit go off." Jesse told him.

"Naw nigga she gotta realize that I'm all she got and she all I got."

"Man, this ain't the way to prove it. You trippin put the gun down."

Daniel starts feeling like his back is against the wall. Then jumps up waving the gun around.

"Nigga choose your side." He pointed the gun at Jesse.

Jesse threw his hands up and shook his head. "We boys. I know the shit but this ain't you. I ain't taking no sides in this shit. I don't want nobody to get killed."

"We been boys for a long time and it looks like you're taking her side now."

Trina pushed the door and to her surprised he started waving the gun around again.

"Baby," Jesse tried to push her back out.

"Well if it ain't the loud mouth of the bunch. Come on in here." He waved the gun in her direction.

Trina looked around and saw Angel lying on the floor, so she immediately started running in her direction until he pointed the gun directly at her.

"Get your ass back!" He yelled. "We don't need no loud mouth heroes in here."

Trina's heart was in her stomach. She had been in crazy situations before but to see the gun pointed directly at her had her blood boiling. A part of her wanted to smack Daniel but she was afraid that he might actually shoot her.

"You ole hoe ass nigga." She mumbled under her breath.

"You better shut the fuck up."

"Make me. If you ain't have that gun in your hands I would whoop you're mutha fuckin ass. Put my pussy in your face and piss on you." She snarled.

"Ooh Jesse you kiss that little dirty mouth of hers? I should blow your brains out."

"Daniel! Nigga put the gun down!" Jesse tried to calm him as Daniel kept waving the gun pointing it at Trina. Jesse ran at him head on. During the scuffle the gun went off hitting Trina in the arm.

"Mutha'fucka you shot my girl!" Jesse screeched.

"It was an accident. You made me do it." Daniel looked around

Jesse ran to Trina. "Nigga I ain't make you do shit."

"You charged at me and made it go off." Looking at the anger in his eyes, Daniel felt like it was them against him. "Fuck that choose your side."

"What? What you mean choose my side? Put the mutha fuckin gun down."

"Oh, okay I see how it is. Pussy over niggas huh? Well say goodbye to your bitch!"

As he pointed the gun right at Trina's head. She turned her head and put her hand out in front of her face. Jesse charged at Daniel again. This time during the scuffle the gun was knocked out of his hand. Without the gun Daniel was no match for Jesse. Daniel tried to get up, but Jesse overpowered him. The two continued to fight until Daniel pulled out a pocket knife and stabbed Jesse. So much was going on that no one knew he was hurt until he fell. Trina cried out to him as he laid there looking at her.

"I'm so tired of hearing this bitch mouth. It ends today."

"Leave her alone mutha'fucka."

Daniel reached for the gun again. Jesse stepped on his hand. Daniel was screaming, and Trina was scuffling to call the police. Angel was still curled up on the floor. Daniel wiggle his hand from under Jesse's foot and reached the gun.

"Y'all got me fucked up." Daniel stood up, pacing back

and forth with the gun. "Y'all really got me fucked up!" he shouted.

There were still five rounds in the gun. He aimed it at Angel and pulled the trigger. Jesse tried to move toward him, but he shot him in the head. Trina was screaming, and he shot her, too. Then, he put the gun to his temple and pulled the trigger. Darkness overcame the room as the quiet settled in. There was nothing be coldness surrounding them while the smell of fresh blood filled the room.

Angel laid there, in a pool of her own blood, hearing the sirens in the distance. She closed her eyes, trying to labor her breath.

"Angel," she heard a faint voice. "Angel? Can you hear me?"

"Yes," she whispered. "Yes, Trina. I can hear you."

"I love you, girl." Trina cried.

Angel closed her eyes and tried to breathe. "I love you too."

The sirens got closer and soon they were surrounded by police and EMT's. One of them recognized them from the drug overdose. Angel looked over at Daniel's lifeless body as they lifted her on the stretcher. Then, she saw Jesse. A tear rolled down her cheek. He had saved her life. As they pushed her toward the ambulance, she was rolled by Trina's stretcher.

"I'm so sorry." She whispered. "I never meant for any of this to happen."

They touched hands for a moment and then were whisked in different directions. Angel was rushed to the emergency room where doctors had to perform surgery on her. She was placed on life support after suffering major blood lost. Trina was hit in the arm and leg. After being released, she and Carla sat by Angel's bedside.

"I wanted you to meet your niece," Carla held the baby by Angel.

The doctors explained that she had minimal brain

function and that if she ever woke up she would be a vegetable. They had held out hope for a few weeks, praying that she would wake up.

"Ms. Jenkins," A doctor came into the room. "You're listed as power of attorney over Ms. Angel Starks."

"Yes," she looked him in the eye.

"Her license lists her as an organ donor." He spoke softly. "We would like you to consider taking her off life support and donating her organs as they can save a lot of people."

Tears fell from Carla's eyes. Trina wrapped her arms around her as they stood there. "Can we have some time to think about it?" Carla asked him.

"Take all the time you need." He left, closing the door.

The two comforted each other as they come to the grim realization that their friend was gone. Carla took a deep breath, trying to think of what Angel would want. It was true that she was listed as an organ donor, but they believed that God would have the final say. She prayed for a clear answer.

"Trina," she looked up. "I think it's time."

"So, do I." she looked over at her friend.

They called the doctor back into the room and informed him of their decision. A nurse came into the room and explained to them what was going to happen. She started to unplug the machine.

"She's comfortable." She assured them. "This could happen quickly or slowly. You all are welcome to stay until she has passed on." She nodded and touched Carla on the shoulder.

She and Trina held Angel's hand and waited. The room was completely silent except for the machines. After about forty minutes she flatlined. Carla and Trina cried out loud.

"Angel…" Trina sighed.

"We love you." They both kissed her on the cheeks.

Donna Plata

Finally, she was at peace.

Made in the USA
Columbia, SC
16 June 2018